BOOK BOYFRIEND BUILDERS

FAKING THE BOOK BOYFRIEND

AK LANDOW

Copyright

Faking the Book Boyfriend

Copyright © 2024 by AK Landow

All rights reserved.

No part of this book may be reproduced in any form or by any electronic or mechanical means, including information storage and retrieval systems, without written permission from the author, except for the use of brief quotations in a book review.

Published by Author AK Landow, LLC

ISBN: 978-1-962575-16-4

Edited and Proofread By: Chrisandra's Corrections

Cover Design By: K.B. Designs

❀ Created with Vellum

Dedication

To my author besties, Jade, Carolina, and L.A. I'm so thankful to you three for your friendship, laughter, kindness, compassion, and perverted sense of humor. You're the cherry on top of the cake of my author journey. Not that kind of cherry. Get your minds out of the gutter, pervs.

"Abandon the cultural myth that all female friendships must be bitchy, toxic, or competitive. This myth is like heels and purses — pretty but designed to SLOW women down."
— Roxane Gay

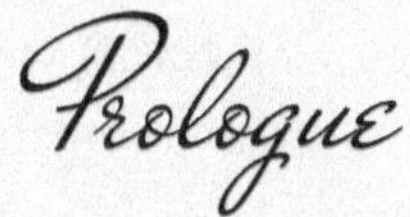

GEMMA

I SLOWLY PEEL my eyes open and inwardly cheer that sunlight is not yet breaking through the tacky, floral hotel curtains. Phew, I don't have to wake up just yet.

I try to move my arm, but my whole body is sore. At the ripe old age of twenty-nine, I can't drink quite like I used to. I hope my face isn't puffy for today's big event. Damn JoJo and her magical mango margaritas.

Despite the ache, the familiar sound of a toilet flushing forces me to roll over. In the darkness, I see Libby making her way out of the bathroom and crawling back into her bed. I grumble, "Fuck, Lib, you pee more often than my ninety-year-old grandfather used to."

She sighs as her long blonde hair falls on the pillow. "Sometimes I wish I was a camel just so I could store it all to sleep through the night. It would be worth having a hairy hump."

"You'd also have a thick, long tongue. I know plenty of men and women who would appreciate that, me included."

She giggles. "You're such a perv."

I yawn and gingerly stretch my arms through a smile. "Proud

of it. And who are you kidding? You're a perv too. That's what makes us good romance authors."

Her hazel eyes sparkle, even in the darkness. "Hmm. Valid point."

I pick up my phone, look at the time, and whine, "Ugh. It's four in the morning. Do you realize there are crazy bitches who wake up at this hour to go workout? I won't even get up to pee. I'd rather lay in pain for three more hours than move right now."

She lets out a laugh. "That's so true. Though I would argue that standing at a book signing for twelve hours in heels in an inadequately air-conditioned room is a workout. I certainly sweat like it's one."

I nod. "You're not wrong. It's a good thing we've got a big book signing today. I guess we'll both look like Jane Fonda by dinnertime."

"Isn't it bizarre that she doesn't age?"

I agree, "Best. Plastic. Surgeon. Ever."

"Too bad she's a communist. It kind of ruins it for me."

I wave my hand dismissively. "Meh. That was a long time ago."

We hear JoJo's voice from the other room. "Will you two shut the fuck up? Ava and I can't sleep with you blabbering about camel-toed commies."

We're sharing a two-bedroom suite with our other author besties, Ava and JoJo.

I shout back. "Sorry. You two go back to cuddling in your bed. Just remember, eating a pussy is like being in the mafia. One slip of the tongue, and you're in deep shit."

Libby and I giggle. Somehow, we were assigned a suite where one bedroom has two queen-sized beds and one has a king. Libby and I won rock-paper-scissors, giving us the better bedroom.

Ava and JoJo both yell, "Fuck you," at the same time.

Libby shakes her head. "You're such an instigator."

I shrug. "I'm nearly thirty. Love me or hate me, I'm not changing at this point."

"*I* love you."

I blow her a kiss. "Love you too, bestie."

It's silent for a moment before she whispers, "I hope I sell fifty books today. According to my financial spreadsheet, I need it to make this trip a success."

I'm concerned for my friend. It isn't the first time she's mentioned money since we've been here. "Why? Is business not going well?"

She recently moved from Texas to Florida for her boyfriend, something I would never in a million years do, and is currently working for herself.

"It's hard doing the freelance web design thing. No consistent paycheck."

"At least you love it. So many people hate what they do. Hell, most lawyers hate their jobs. I'm the exception. I know I'm lucky that my boss is awesome and supportive of my writing side gig, but I wish being an author paid better so I could have more balance in my life. Maybe even find someone to share it with."

She blows out a breath. "I guess writing is more of a labor of love for us."

I nod. "It is. One day we'll all be as big and awesome as TL Swan."

"That's the dream."

"Speaking of which, we should get some more beauty sleep. We've got a long day ahead of us."

"You're right. Night, Gem."

"Night, Lib."

I WAKE to a sunlit room and the toilet flushing. I mumble, "Again, Lib?"

She shrugs. "Twenty-seven is the new eighty-seven."

"I think it's supposed to be the other way around."

"It's time to get up anyway. Will you...umm...do my makeup today?"

My eyebrows must shoot into my hairline. Libby rarely cares about that kind of stuff. "I'd be happy to. Any particular reason?"

"You're so good at it, and you're always perfectly put together." She wiggles her tall, skinny frame. "I need a little of that sassy, classy lady energy today."

I smile in realization. "Ahh. I forgot that Riggs Romero will be appearing at our signing."

Riggs is a famous romance novel cover model. Libby has had a crush on him for as long as I can remember.

She blushes.

I don't want to embarrass her further. I'm happy she asked for my help. "I'd love to do your makeup."

I head into the bathroom to brush my teeth. She yells from the bedroom, "That buzzing noise better be an electric toothbrush, not a vibrator. You have forty color-coded bottles in there and I'm afraid to ask what half of them are. And straighten them up. You know I hate disorder."

She's a neat freak.

With a mouth full of toothpaste, I mumble, "It's a toothbrush. I only use my vibrator in bed after you fall asleep—while I gaze at you."

She starts laughing. "You're such a degenerate."

I smile. I adore Libby and treasure the once or twice a year we get to hang out together. With me living in Philadelphia and her now in Florida, we only see each other at book signings that we both attend.

After I finish in the bathroom, I start her makeup. Letting out a moan, I declare, "Your cheekbones are model-like. I barely need to use any blush."

She bats her eyelashes. "That's me. Famous supermodel. My milkshake brings all the boys to the yard." She shimmies a bit.

"Speaking of bringing boys to the yard, any worthwhile dates lately?"

I sigh. "Not really. I was on one last week where the guy talked about his car for sixty straight minutes. I couldn't get a single word in. He didn't ask me any questions about my life. Some guys are such boneheads. They don't know how to behave on dates. They have no clue what women want."

"Why didn't you get up and leave?"

I've been known to do that if a date is going poorly. Why waste anyone's time when you know nothing will progress?

I scrunch my nose. "Aiden was at the same restaurant."

She nods in understanding. Aiden is my ex-boyfriend. We broke up about six months ago, and he loves parading his new assortment of women in front of me all the time.

"I didn't want him to see me on a bad date, so I laughed and pretended to be interested in car mechanics. It might actually be the most boring topic on the planet. The more I laughed about things that weren't funny, the more my date droned on and on about them."

Just then, JoJo and Ava walk into our room. I let out a whistle. "Wow. You two look gorgeous."

JoJo is a little younger than me. Her dirty blond hair is straightened, and her trademark black outfit doesn't mask her gorgeous curves.

Ava is the oldest of all of us, with brown hair, blue eyes, and curves that match JoJo's. She's a stunner.

Ava gives us a bashful smile, but JoJo sucks in her cheeks. "I do look like Giselle, don't I? I hope my karate instructor wants to bang me like hers did."

Libby channels her best Marilyn Monroe voice, and breathes, "Yes, sensei. Your wood is so big and hard, sensei. You bring me to my knees, sensei. How about I show you how far I can spread my legs, sensei?"

We all burst out laughing as JoJo places a coffee carrier with four cups on the desk.

Libby looks at it. "Did you get any cream and sugar?"

JoJo lifts an eyebrow. "They're already in your coffees. You like one cream and two-and-a-half sugars. Two isn't enough and three is too many. Ava likes it black. Gemma likes a splash of skim milk. Not a full pour because then it makes her coffee cold."

I love that she knows all that.

She hands me mine and I take a sip. "Yum. This is good. Where's it from?"

JoJo is a coffee snob. She refuses to drink hotel lobby coffee and always brings her own coffee grounds to brew when she travels.

"This little gourmet shop near my house. Fucking TSA always thinks I'm trafficking drugs when I fly with my coffee grounds. I usually get pulled to the side and they check it. That's not even why I got pulled aside before a flight a few weeks ago though. Note to self, don't travel through airport metal detectors in a bodysuit that has a metal clasp at the crotch. I think Vernon from TSA is the most action I've gotten in months."

Libby quips, "That sounds like a reason you *should* wear a bodysuit through the airport. Was Vernon hot?"

JoJo shakes her head. "Vernon was so ugly he could scare the crap out of a toilet. When he looks in the mirror, the reflection walks away."

Ava spits out her coffee in laughter. "Oh my god. That's horrible…and hysterical."

I nod in agreement as I quickly type away on my phone. "I agree that it's horrible and hysterical. It's now going in my next book. Thanks, JoJo."

She sarcastically responds, "Nothing says rom-com like a good old-fashioned airport near-fingerfucking incident."

I smile as I turn Libby toward the mirror to show her my finished product. "Liberty Hill, meet your alter ego, Libby Cocks *in your mouth*, banter queen of the south."

She rolls her eyes. "My pen name is Libby Cox with an *x*, not Cocks as in dicks."

I wink. "Potato, pat*ahto*."

She takes in her full reflection and gasps. "Oh, Gem, even with only one eye I can see what a great job you did." Libby is blind in her left eye and always makes jokes about it.

After everyone agrees, Libby and I finish getting dressed and meet JoJo and Ava in the living room of our suite.

Ava sighs. "Let's rock this and sell some books. I didn't fly all the way to Colorado with this shit just to have to take it all home with me."

We all grab our oversized trunks of books that we travel with and then make our way to the convention hall for the giant book signing.

FOURTEEN HOURS LATER

We're all lounging in our pajamas in the living room of our suite, braless, makeup-less, and in a Chinese food coma. We're drinking some weird JoJo-produced wine and vodka concoction that I know will lead us in a bad direction, but I love these girls and we're having too much fun to let a little thing like the promise of a bad hangover deter us from a good time.

Our normal silliness is broken up by Libby admitting that she and her boyfriend, Logan, broke up. I feel so bad for her. She moved halfway across the country for that dickhead.

And then Ava admits that her man-child ex-husband, Zach, still calls her because he doesn't know how to manage his own life.

I sigh. "What does it say about us that we write romance yet can't seem to find men who come close to the ones we write about? Do you think our standards are too high?"

Ava shakes her head. "Absolutely not. We just haven't found

the right guys yet. They're out there. Don't give up on finding your Mr. Perfect."

"Ahhh, Mr. Perfect. What does he look like?"

Libby smirks. "He's tall, tattooed, has bulging muscles, a six-pack, and a dick so big, when he's hard, it causes a solar eclipse."

We all laugh as I shake my head. "I didn't mean that question literally. I meant it more figuratively. How does he treat us? How do we want him to treat us? Isn't it more about how he makes you feel? If he makes you feel like his queen, that's a *Mr. Perfect.*"

Ava, always the retrospective one, says, "I hear what you're saying. I loved Zach, but being married to him didn't make me feel good."

Libby quips, "Because you were more like a babysitter, not a wife."

I nod. "Exactly. There's some woman out there who has an over-the-top maternal urge. She *wants* a man like Zach to depend on her. He will make *her* feel good, he just didn't make *you* feel good, Ava."

JoJo scoffs. "I feel like Zach is one of those weird fuckers who likes to wear diapers and be mommied as a kink."

Ava's mouth widens. "Is that a thing?"

Libby answers, "It sure is. I was in the rabbit hole of googling kinks the other day to see if there are any I haven't used yet, and that one came up. It's not sexy. At. All."

I remark, "But some kinky bitch out there is into it. That makes Zach *her* Mr. Perfect."

We all yap about weird kinks for a while. You can have frank conversations like this with your author friends that you can't always have with your real-life friends. It's bizarre. We talk about the finer intricacies of anal sex like we're discussing our grocery lists.

I love these ladies. We only met a few years ago online, but they've become so damn special to me. We text in our group chat every single day. Some bookish topics, and some not-so-bookish topics. We'd probably be arrested in a few states if those text chains ever saw the light of day.

After a few more rounds of drinks and a hilarious incident where Libby accidentally used my lube as hand lotion, we somehow get back to talking about Mr. Perfect. A thought occurs to me. "There needs to be some kind of boot camp for guys where they're trained to be book boyfriends."

Libby, being the jokester, starts on about what the boot camp would entail. Teaching hopeless men things like the art of sexy doorframe leans, telling us we're good girls, proper growling technique, and my personal favorite, which I've never admitted to anyone, possessiveness. Some people are turned off by it, but there's a reason I write about possessive men. I've never truly had one, and I know, deep down inside, I want one.

They're joking about boot camp shenanigans and calling Libby a drill sergeant, but I think there's something to it. I'm quiet for a bit, not listening to whatever it is they're saying before I chime in, "Ya know, it's not that bad of an idea."

Libby appears confused. "What's not a bad idea?"

I take a long sip of the weird shit we're drinking that I can no longer taste, before answering, "Training men to become book boyfriends."

JoJo says, "Well, yeah. That would be nice. Someone needs to do something with the current dating pool. It's abysmal."

I look at all of them. "Just hear me out. What if *we* started a business to do that?"

Ava laughs. "You want to turn Drill Sergeant Libby loose on the men of America? Ooh! Can we get her a whip?"

They're all laughing, but I'm dead serious. At least I think I am. "Maybe not boot camp style—though I would love to see Libs wield a whip on some clueless sap—but why couldn't we be consultants? We write the kind of men women want, so why couldn't we be hired to...*educate* guys?"

Libby responds, "But then some poor girl gets stuck with a man who's just pretending."

I emphatically shake my head. "No, not like that. We'd want them to be their authentic selves but simply a better version. Teach them how to be more thoughtful. How to cater to their woman's needs." I look at JoJo. "Like when you knew our coffee preferences this morning. I dated Aiden for years, and he was still clueless about how I take my coffee. And I order the same damn thing every time."

Libby pinches her eyebrows together. "Sooo, you want to help men learn their woman's coffee orders?"

I sigh. They're not taking me seriously. "Among other things. I think there are a lot of good men out there, but some are clueless about a lot of things. But they wouldn't be if they would just *pay attention* to their woman's needs. We could give them the tools they need to do that. To read verbal and non-verbal clues."

JoJo's entire face lights up. "You know, that might actually work. It's definitely an untapped market with lots of potential."

I see Ava deep in thought before something occurs to her. "Ooh, I have a friend who reads my books with her boyfriend. She said their relationship has really improved a lot since they started, and not just in the bedroom. She thinks it inspired him or something."

Libby suggests using our romance books as marketing manuals, but I shake my head. "Not exactly what I was thinking. We should provide an actual service to clients who are interested."

She asks, "And charge people for it?"

I see in JoJo's face that she now understands what I'm getting at. "Yeah, I imagine a lot of women would enroll their boyfriends in the…what would it be? An online course?"

Ava shakes her head. "It would be more personal if we met the clients face-to-face."

Libby toggles her head and finger around at all of us. "Y'all are talking like we're actually going to do this."

JoJo challenges, "Why shouldn't we? Who better to help men become book boyfriends than romance authors? We know all the tricks. And just think about how many women it would help.

They could turn their man into their *dream man* with a little advice from four authors who know a thing or two about what women want."

Libby considers it for a moment. "True. We all get tons of messages and reviews from readers saying they wish they could find a man like the ones in our books."

I nod. "And though we write our men as uber attractive, I guarantee ninety percent of those women are more interested in how the book boyfriends *act* than their physical appearance." I feel tears welling in my eyes as it becomes a bit more personal for me. "Every woman wants to be treated with the respect she deserves."

Something Aiden never truly gave me. Libby knows this and offers me a hug before asking, "You really think we can do it?"

I swallow back my tears and smile. "Fuck yeah we can. I think it could be something really great. We all bring unique talents to the table. Lib, you can whip us up a website in minutes." I look at Ava. "You're a marketing genius. You and JoJo," who's in PR, "can get our business seen on every cell phone in this country. In the world!"

I see the corners of JoJo's lips raise. "Gem, you can make sure everything is legal. This is fucking brilliant. I'm all in. Let's do this."

Ava blows out a breath. "Are you guys cool showing your faces?"

We all nod that we are.

"Good. Cause, TBH, we're kinda hotties, and I think we should record a few videos about this new endeavor. We'll spread them around on social media. I have a few tricks up my sleeve to get them seen right away. And JoJo makes amazing videos. We'll both make a few."

I mumble, "Then make my fucking books hit on TikTok, dammit."

Ava giggles. "Not even Einstein could crack the BookTok code. But this? This is right in my wheelhouse."

We scramble for a long while, each working copiously on our respective roles. I look around at my friends and smile. They're so into it.

At some point, we're ready to go live. JoJo looks at Libby and nods her head. "Activate the website."

Libby makes a slow show of pressing the button on her laptop.

We all immediately share our various creations across our social media accounts. I can't believe we actually did this. "That may have been the most idiotic thing we've ever done."

Libby scowls at me. "It was your idea."

She does make a good point.

We continue to laugh about the advice we'd give men and drink until we can't see straight. The last thing I remember before passing out is us all clinking glasses and yelling, "To the Book Boyfriend Builders!"

CHAPTER

One

I SMILE into my phone as I look at my niece, Maggie's, adorable little freckled face and messy brown hair. "Sorry I had to leave your T-ball game early today, but I saw your homerun. You're a chip off the old block."

"Uncle Twey," she can't pronounce her blended R's yet, "Mommy said I hit like her, not you."

I hear my sister, Diana, laughing in the background before she yells, "It's true, Magpie. I was always a better hitter than Uncle Trey."

I twist my lips. "Hmm, that might be a little true, at least when I was four, like you, Magpie. Your mommy was six, so she was bigger and stronger than I was. She was a very good ballplayer."

Maggie gives me one of her sweet smiles. "Will you come to another game? All the parents on the team were excited you were there. My fwiend Jenna said you're famous. I told her it wasn't twue, but she asked if she could have your autogwaph."

I chuckle. She's so freakin' cute. "Of course your friend can have my autograph. I'll bring Bombers' stuff for everyone on your team. If you want me at your next game, I'll be there, baby girl."

"Yay! Thanks, Uncle Twey. I gotta go eat my veggies so I can have ice cweam tonight. Mommy wants to talk to you."

"Okay. Love you, Magpie."

"Love you too, Uncle Twey-pie."

My sister takes the phone. Her familiar blue eyes meet mine as she holds her baby boy, Leo. "Thanks for being there today. She was excited to see you. She never realized that you're famous, but all the parents were chatting about it after the game. Now Maggie thinks you're a movie star."

I straighten my collar on the nice shirt I'm wearing. "That's how I roll." I wink. "It must be my movie star good looks."

"Don't get a big head. You'll always be Demon Trey to me."

I wince at the nod to my real first name, DeMontré, which no one knows. Ever since I was old enough to offer an opinion, I've gone by Trey. My big sister loved to call me Demon Trey instead.

Leo coos, "Demon, demon, demon."

What? He's not even one yet. "Is he talking?"

She shrugs. "He mimics all the time. I have to watch my mouth around him, Demon Trey."

"Shh. Layton and Cheetah are here. I don't want them to ever find out my real first name. They'll never let me live it down."

"Riiight. Your big dinner tonight. That's why you had to head home early. I'll let you go."

"It's okay. Those prima donnas are still getting dressed."

She grins before her face turns more serious. "Hey, I'm sorry you lost in the playoffs, but I'm happy you have some free time. We all hope to see you more often. Maggie adores you. She's at a fun age right now."

"I adore her too. It was exciting to see her play." This fall was her first season being old enough to play T-ball, and it's the first game I've been able to attend due to my busy baseball schedule. "Honestly, Lady Di, she's the best. You're an amazing mom."

She smiles. "Thank you. I hope you have one while you're still young enough to enjoy them. Any prospects?"

I shake my head. "Just the usual groupies. It's hard to find a good woman. You set the bar too high."

She rolls her eyes. "You're full of shit, but I appreciate the compliment. And I get how hard it is for you. Stay away from the bloodsuckers."

"I'm trying."

"I worry about you."

"Don't. When the right girl comes along, I'll know."

"I hope you're looking in the right places."

I'm not, so I don't bother to answer. "I need to run."

She sighs. "Okay. I'm really sorry for what Tanner is going through. Give him my best."

"Will do."

I hang up the phone and yell out from the living room. "Are you jerkoffs ready? You two take longer to get dressed than chicks."

My friends Layton Lancaster and Cruz "Cheetah" Gonzales are staying with me in my New York City penthouse for the night. I play professional baseball for the New York Bombers and they both play for the Philadelphia Cougars. We all share the same agent, Tanner Montgomery. His divorce became finalized this week, and he's a bit down. We're taking him out to a steak dinner to both celebrate the end of a long, draining process and cheer him up.

Layton walks out of one of my guestrooms and smooths the sides of his brown hair with both hands. "You can't rush perfection, DePaul." He points to his body as he swivels his hips. "The ladies love the whole package. They all want to be *#laidbylayton.*"

Pathetically, *#laidbylayton* is often used on social media by women Layton beds and plenty of women he doesn't. It's always a trending hashtag and he loves to rub it in our faces.

Cheetah then walks out of the room he's using. "Lancaster, you're practically deformed with your weirdly square chin. No woman in her right mind wants that."

Layton deadpans, "Do you even comprehend how many women clamor to sit on this chin? They fucking dream about it."

Cheetah chuckles. "You're such a douchebag. In fact, you graduated come loudly from Douchebag University."

I ask, "Cum Laude, as in graduating with honors?"

Cheetah thumps his head. "In my mind, it's come loudly. I graduated from StudMan U with a degree in making women come loudly."

I sigh. "You're both the co-valedictorians of Douchebag University. Can we go now? Lancaster will cause a paparazzi shitstorm. It's going to take us twice as long to get there."

While Cheetah and I are recognized within our respective playing towns of Philadelphia and New York City, Layton is one of the most popular players in all of baseball and has been for over a decade. He's recognized everywhere he goes and can't go anywhere without being hounded by autograph seekers and people with cameras begging for a picture of him, often with his latest conquest.

AN HOUR LATER, we're sitting at a table with Tanner as we all sip high-end whiskey from our whiskey tumblers and feast on a fresh seafood tower ahead of our steaks arriving. Tanner looks like shit, with bags under his eyes. He rubs his dark beard before admitting, "I feel like I've failed Harper. She's only three. She won't even remember the time period in her life when Fallon and I were together."

The three of us look at each other. We can't offer much

guidance. None of us are fathers and none of us have been married. Layton and I are probably among the older unmarried players in the league. He's thirty, and I'm twenty-nine. Even Cheetah, at twenty-seven, is an older unmarried man in our league. Many of the guys marry young, most to their high school sweethearts. I get the appeal of that. Someone who cared about you *before* you had money. *Before* you were famous. That's priceless.

He continues, "And now I only get her half the time."

I pinch my lips together. "I'm sorry, man. Divorce sucks. My parents went through it. If it makes you feel better, I remember their last few months together, and it would have been better for me if I didn't."

He slowly nods. "I suppose. I'm trying to keep things civil with Fallon. It's better for Harper. That's why I asked you guys to dinner tonight."

Cheetah, who has looked at his phone ten times since we've been here, feigns hurt. "It wasn't for our wit and charm?"

Tanner clears his throat. "Definitely not."

Cheetah wiggles his hips in his seat. "My Latino flair?"

"Umm, no. In all sincerity, you three mean a lot to me. You're the first three clients I called when I left SMI and went out on my own because you're like family to me. None of you asked any questions or hesitated. You blindly followed me. I can't tell you how much that meant." He swallows down his obvious emotions. "As you may know, Fallon is originally from Philadelphia. She moved here after grad school, and then we met and eventually got married. But she wants to move home now, closer to her family, and I understand why."

Layton pinches his eyebrows together. "Does that mean Harper will have to split time between Philly and New York?"

Tanner shakes his head. "That's not fair to Harper. I don't want her wasting her childhood in a car or train. And I don't want to miss her eventual school and sporting events." He briefly pauses, pushing his lips together in a thin line. "I'm moving to Philly. Effective next week, Montgomery Sports Management will be headquartered in Philadelphia."

I'm hit with a sudden wave of emotion. I've always had Tanner nearby, ever since I was an eighteen-year-old kid getting drafted by the Bombers. Even though he's only ten years older, he's been a surrogate father to me in this crazy city. I can't fathom being here without him.

I put my own fears aside and slap his back, giving him the reinforcement I know he needs right now. "I'll miss having you here, but I understand. Family first. I commend you for putting Harper's needs and happiness above your own. You're a great father."

He smiles in gratitude, knowing I'm the most adversely affected of the three of us. Layton appears thrilled that he'll have Tanner nearby. I know he, too, looks to Tanner as a father figure in his life, not having a father of his own.

I glance over at Cheetah who is looking at his phone again. It's annoying me. Tanner needs us, and Cheetah is only half listening.

I bark, "Cheetah! What is so damn important that you're on your phone during our friend's time of need?"

His blue eyes snap up toward Tanner. "Sorry. I know moving isn't ideal, but I'd be lying if I said I wasn't thrilled to have you in Philly."

I nod toward his phone. "What's going on?"

"Just a funny situation online that I can't stop watching. It's been unfolding all day."

Tanner sighs. "I could use a distraction. I know I'm the Grim Reaper tonight. Tell us what it is. But if it's porn, I don't need to hear about it."

Layton and I smile at each other. Cheetah is known for watching a ton of porn. He doesn't bother to hide it.

Cheetah points to his phone. "These four hot chicks—not trashy hot, classy hot—clearly had too much to drink last night. They're all romance book authors, and they posted videos of their new business. It's called Book Boyfriend Builders. They train men to act like the men in their novels."

I ask, "Like in the books you read?"

Cheetah reads romance novels all the time.

He nods. "Yes. I've actually read some of their books. I never knew what the authors looked like. They're hot as hell. They posted last night, and they have tens of thousands of comments. Some of them are a riot."

I scroll through a few of them on his phone.

"Romance novels, huh?" Layton mock sways long hair that he doesn't have. "Like Fabio riding a horse at sunset?"

Cheetah lets out a loud laugh. "Fabio is, like, eighty now. Maybe forty years ago. But sort of. He was a fantasy to women, and now these authors want to teach you how to become a fantasy man. They're calling it a man training academy." In a female voice, he breathes, "You, too, can be as sexy as the famous Layton Lancaster. If you have a square chin and take lessons from us, women will beg to sit on your face like they do for Layton."

Tanner and Layton are doubled over in laughter. I nod toward Cheetah's phone. "Let's see the video."

He turns his phone and presses the button. It is, in fact, four drunk women growling at and spanking each other. They keep calling one another good girls and then giggling uncontrollably.

They're in pajamas, holding drinks. He's right that they're all attractive, but it's the brunette with big green eyes and full lips in the dark pink, silk pajamas who catches my eye. Her hair is up in a bun, but pieces fall on her gorgeous face. Even in the loose pajamas, I can see she's got a great body. She's effortlessly sexy as hell. Everything she does and every giggle she makes has my heart beating faster.

I point at her. "What's her name? She's fucking beautiful."

I can't stop staring at her. Every move she makes seems so unintentionally erotic, from licking her lips to moving pieces of her hair off her face. My mouth is watering.

Cheetah shrugs. "I only know her pen name, not her real name. It's Tami Maida."

I can't help but smile at the pop culture reference. I look around at the guys, realizing that the name doesn't register on their faces. This chick is clever.

He continues, "I read one of her books. It takes place in Philadelphia. All of her books do. I think that's where she lives."

I try to play it cool. "So...umm...what happens if you sign up for her...their service?"

Layton scoffs. "You pull nearly as much ass as I do, DePaul. Why the hell would you need this service? Chicks flock to your all-American looks and dented ass-crack chin."

Cheetah rolls his eyes. "Lancaster, you're a fuckwit. He's not interested in the service. He's interested in the sexy woman providing the service."

Cheetah turns to Tanner and scrunches his face. "Sorry, man. We don't need to talk about hot chicks right now."

It's undeniable that Fallon Montgomery is an extremely attractive woman.

Tanner bites off a piece of shrimp with nothing but a big smile on his face. "This is a great distraction for me. No need to further wallow in my misery. Let's sign him up. This is much more fun than me talking about my divorce."

Cheetah's face lights up. "Alright. You good with that, DePaul?"

I pretend to consider it, even though I was already planning to do it as soon as I got home. I nonchalantly shrug. "Sure. Why not?"

He presses a few buttons and mindlessly says, "Name... Trey DeP—"

I interrupt. "Don't use my real full name. I don't want her to know I play ball."

They all understand that. It's sometimes hard for us to let people in, not knowing their intentions. That's why we rarely find ourselves in relationships. Women are interested in our notoriety more than anything remotely substantive.

"Oooo-kay. What name?"

"What are the next few questions?"

"Where do you live and what do you do for a living?"

"Let's work backward. Obviously, write that I live in Philly, so she has more incentive to take me on as a client. What's a humble profession?"

He twists his lips. "Hmm. I don't know. A teacher?"

"No, that's too specific. She'll ask which school and shit. Pick something else."

Cheetah thinks for a moment. "Porn star?"

"Pass."

Layton's face brightens. "What about a plumber?"

Cheetah nods. "Yes, you can unclog her pipes."

I consider it for a moment. "That might work. Now google plumbers in Philly named Trey, just in case she googles me. Preferably a last name that starts with D."

Cheetah fumbles on his phone for a minute. "There's a Trey Donatucci's Plumbing company."

I smile. "Perfect. Trey Donatucci it is."

He continues to input my information. "Hobbies?"

"Write *football*, both playing and watching." They may not get the Tami Maida reference, but I do.

"Okay. What about a personal statement of why they should consider working with you?"

I grab his phone. "I'll type it."

I spend a few minutes doing so before he reads it with a smile. "That's perfect. Now we need two pictures. They want one that shows your physical appearance and another that shows your personality." He glances at me with a confused look on his face. "A picture that shows your personality?"

I shrug. "Maybe a funny photo or one of me doing a hobby?"

"If she sees your photo, she may know who you are."

"I don't think my face is as recognizable as Lancaster's outside of New York, especially for a woman from Philly." I rub my scruff. "And I have more facial hair than I normally do."

Our team owner forbids facial hair during the season, but we're in the off-season now and I can do what I want.

The waiter comes by and asks if we need drink refills. Tanner answers that we do. An idea occurs to me. I look up at the waiter. "Hey man, do you have a hat and sunglasses I can borrow?"

His face lights up with excitement. "I have a Bombers hat, Mr. DePaul."

"Anything but Bombers. A football team would be perfect. Or a knit hat would be even better. Not a baseball cap."

His face falls. "Give me a minute. I'll see what I can come up with from the employee locker room."

"Thank you. And I'd be happy to sign your Bombers hat if you'd like."

He grins like he just won the lottery. "I would be honored. Thank you, sir."

After a brief hat signing and a few photos, I'm wearing a knit hat and sunglasses. Cheetah takes a picture of my profile, not from the front, just in case.

He looks down at his phone. "Damn, Trey, you're a hottie. Don't worry, you can't make out the butthole in your chin."

Layton and Tanner once again burst out in laughter. They all love to make fun of my chin dimple.

I roll my eyes. "Now I need a personality photo. Any ideas?"

We all think as our steaks are served and we begin to slice into the juicy goodness. Cheetah chews but I can tell he's thinking long and hard about it.

"Ooh. I have an idea. Trey, stand and bend over."

"No, I will not bend over for you."

"Just do it. It will be funny."

I stand in my black jeans and sweater and then turn around. I bend over slightly, and he snaps a photo.

After sitting back down, I see him typing furiously on his phone. I motion my hand toward it. "What did you write?"

"Under a photo of your covered ass, which is sexy by the way, I wrote, *No plumber's crack here, but I do promise to crack you up. The only pipes I'll make burst are yours.*"

I smile. "Perfect. Submit it. Game on, *Tami Maida*."

CHAPTER

Two

GEMMA

IT'S SUNDAY NIGHT, and I'm flying home from our book signing. We were supposed to stay until tomorrow but there's a big storm coming in, so I grabbed a late-night flight to get out of Colorado ahead of it.

We woke up hungover as all hell with completely flooded inboxes and social media posts that went viral. Our drunken business creation completely exploded while we slept. Apparently, thousands of men want to learn how to be like romance book boyfriends.

I've downed about twenty glasses of water and have eaten the greasiest food you can imagine. I'm ready to get to work going through all the applications. I open my laptop, completely dumbfounded by the number of applicants.

The four of us agreed that we would each take at least one client immediately to see how it goes. Libby and Ava mentioned taking on more than one, but with my demanding job and my writing, I don't have time for more than one man.

We want to give this business a go, having nothing to lose except a little time. We also decided that it makes the most sense to take on clients near where we live so we can meet with them in person as we learn how to navigate our way through this new business.

I love the idea, but I'm not optimistic that this business will be sustainable. If I'm only doing this once, I want a good guy who genuinely wants and needs my help.

I'm able to filter all the applications for those living in or near Philadelphia. There are several dozen of them.

I start carefully reading through all the answers to our questions, hoping to find the right man.

Wow, some of these guys are super weird. Several of them basically admit that it's to get into women's pants. Morons.

There are many others who are interested in *us* because of our videos, not in learning to be book boyfriends. *Pass.*

Then there are a lot of guys who clearly have no chance of ever getting into women's pants. I'll pass on those too.

I'm losing hope until I come across an answer that immediately catches my eye:

Dear Quarterback Princess:

*I'm sure your inbox is **flooded** right now with men wanting your help. It's a good thing that I'm a plumber and managing floods is my specialty.*

*Sometimes it's **draining** for me to find the right woman. I think it's **crap** that they're focused on my job and not on me.*

*Admittedly, sometimes I **crack** under pressure. That's why I need a **service call** from you. My **pipe** dream is to find someone who loves me, complete with all my **leaks**. I'm hoping you can **unclog** the dating pool for me with your wisdom.*

*I have faith that the world is **flush** with amazing women, but I'm asking for your help to make them see the real me.*

Sincerely,
*Willing to Take the **Plunge***

I can't help but giggle. This guy is clever. Let me look at his picture.

Hmm. It's only his profile, and he's oddly in a hat and glasses, but he's not bad looking. It's weird that he covered up though. I wonder what he's trying to hide.

But then I look at his second shot and start laughing hysterically, earning myself a disapproving look from the woman sitting next to me on the plane.

Okay, the plumber is funny, and, if nothing else, he has a great ass.

I think his personal statement alone sets him apart from the other men. This is the guy I want to help.

I pull up the email address he left and let him know that I'm taking him on as a client. I suggest meeting at a local bar that's usually quiet during the after-work hours, asking that he pick the day.

WHEN I'M in the Uber on the way home from the airport, I decide to call my grandmother who lives in Florida. I haven't spoken with her since last week. We're extremely close, rarely letting more than a few days go by without talking.

She never sleeps so I know she'll be up at this late hour.

It's always a FaceTime call with her. She loves seeing my face, and I love seeing hers.

She answers after a few rings with only her forehead visible, per normal. She can't figure out how to accept a call and have her face in the frame all at the same time.

"Ms. Gemma Morgan Fairchild, is that you?"

I smile at her using my full name. "Yes, Grammy Jane Ellen Rockefeller." Her full name.

I see her fumble for her glasses and come into full view as she grins at me. Her green eyes that match mine meet my gaze with warmth. "There's my beautiful granddaughter."

I take in my amazing grandmother who I know is exactly what I'll look like in fifty years. Her no longer naturally dark hair is in a perfect chignon, as always. I ask, "How are you, my beautiful grandmother?"

"Well, I woke up at three a.m. today with a leg cramp. Then I sneezed and threw out my back. I'm one fart away from being paralyzed."

My eyes tear as I burst out in laughter. The Uber driver briefly glares at me. "Grammy Jane, that's the funniest thing I've heard in a long time. I'm using that in a book."

She pumps her fist. "Yes! Put me in the acknowledgments as G.I. Jane."

"You know I always do."

She loves coming up with one-liners for my books. She equally loves it when I acknowledge her as G.I. Jane, which is, oddly, her favorite movie.

She winks. "Guess what? Happy read one of your books." Happy is the nickname for her friend, Harriet. "She told me to tell you that you should add a warning at the beginning of them to make sure our vibrators have full batteries. Apparently, there was an incident where she was walking around naked in her apartment looking for batteries after reading a steamy scene. Samuel was driving by in his cart. He saw her in the window and drove off the road, tipping his cart over."

I gasp. "Oh my god. Is he okay?"

"Just a few cuts and bruises. He'll be fine."

"I'm glad to hear it. I suppose a warning is something to consider for the future. I don't want poor Samuel to get hurt again."

"Happy said she was excited that her saggy boobs had such an impact on him. She's been trying to bed Samuel for months. This may have done the trick."

"Thrilled to have helped your sixty-five-plus community continue its reputation of having the highest rate of STDs in the state."

She giggles. "Damn straight. Proud of it."

"No doubt. How was Mom's visit?"

My mother visited her last week. The two of them often butt heads. I tend to be the referee between them, but I didn't join my mother on her visit due to my book signing.

Grammy Jane moans in malcontent.

"Be nice. She's your daughter."

"Sometimes I question if she's really mine. She thinks she's Jackie Kennedy and the Queen of England all in one. Apparently, she requires royal treatment when coming here and didn't appreciate that I refused to roll out the red carpet for her."

I smile. "That's true, she does like living in luxury. Did she mention the new man she's seeing? I met him once. He seemed…nice."

Grammy Jane makes a gagging face. "Ad nauseam. He called every five minutes. She must be good in the sack. It's the one and only thing she got from me."

I giggle. "Let's hope your good genetics carry through for generations. And don't be mean to her. Some daughters don't visit their mothers at all."

"True. Mortimer and Millie's kids never visit."

"There you go. At least Mom makes time for you."

"But she's no fun. Not like you. She wouldn't drink margaritas and had a fit when I wanted to eat off paper plates. Then she started whining about your books."

I sigh. Mom doesn't support my writing like Grammy Jane does. "It's okay. Not everyone understands this passion. A lot of my close friends don't get it either."

"She hasn't even read them all. She calls them *sex books*. I told her how wonderful your stories are, but she worries that you spend your evenings writing when you should be spending them out socializing. She's very focused on you finding a man, as if it should be your sole focus in life."

"Honestly, she's not wrong about my lack of socializing. Since I started writing, I don't go out as much as I used to."

I make a quick mental note to go out a little more than I have been for the past six months.

"Your happiness matters. Anyone with half a brain can see that writing makes you happy. And when it comes to matters of the heart, you can't force these things. The right person will come along at the right time. I think it's wonderful that you create love stories and put yourself out there like that. It takes courage, and I'm proud of you."

My heart fills with warmth for my number one fan. "Thank you. I appreciate your support. Honestly, Mom's comments don't bother me anymore. Some people support my writing and some don't. I like having this separate identity. I love the bookish community."

"I know you do. How was the signing? Were there any sexy cover models there?"

"It went well. It was good to see my author friends. I sold a bunch of books. And yes, there were a few cover models. One of my author friends has a crush on Riggs Romero. He's a hottie."

Grammy Jane moans. "Umm hmm. He's finger-licking yummy. Did you bed any of them?"

I let out a laugh. "No, none of them are my type."

"Your type might require a makeover."

I think of my last two boyfriends. "Hmm. You're not wrong."

"Don't let your mother tell you what kind of man to date. You need a man without a pole up his ass like that last guy. What was his name?"

"Aiden."

"Yes, there's no way he did it for you. And who was the snooze fest before him? The man you were seeing while you were in law school."

"Sterling."

"Oh god, yes. What a pretentious name. That sounds like someone your mother would date. You weren't…yourself with those guys. They both tried to make you someone you're not."

Leave it to Granny Jane to hit the nail on the head.

She continues, "I want you to find a man who will give you laugh lines when you're as old as me, is proud of you, who values your happiness, who always takes your breath away, and you equally take his breath away. A man who loves you exactly as you are. It wouldn't hurt if he was good in the sack too. Find someone who checks *all* the boxes. Don't *ever* settle for less."

"Like you and Grampy?"

She smiles as if she's remembering my grandfather who died nearly two decades ago. "Yes. When the right man comes along, you won't be able to fathom life without him. I promise."

"Let's hope he exists."

"He does. When will I see your gorgeous face in person?"

"I'll be down to visit in a few weeks. I'm so excited to spend Christmas with you. It's already cold in Philly. I can't wait to hang by the pool with you and your ladies."

"Oh yes. They've all got ideas for your next book."

"I bet they do." Every time I visit, her friends pitch me ideas. It's like they get off on their stories possibly appearing in my books.

"I'll fire up the margarita machine."

"Perfect. And you'll be nice to Mom, right?"

"As long as she's nice to you."

"Fair enough. Love you, Grammy Jane."

"Love you too, beautiful Gemma Morgan."

As soon as we hang up, my email pings with a new mail notification. It's Trey Donatucci. That was fast. He's asking to meet tomorrow evening at the bar I suggested.

CHAPTER

GEMMA

IT'S MONDAY MORNING, and I'm in my office. My boss pokes her pretty face in the door. "Hi, Gemma. I didn't think I'd see you today. I thought you were traveling?"

"There was a weather system coming in, so I left a day early. I got back into town last night."

She scoffs. "And you still came to work?"

"If I have no good reason to fall behind, then why bother?"

"Hmm. I suppose that's why you're one of my top ten favorite employees."

I raise an eyebrow at her, and she giggles. There are only ten people working in this small law practice.

Darian Lawrence Knight is the best boss a girl could ever hope for. She's semi-retired and only comes into the office one or two days a week. After training me in corporate law, she turned over the reins to me and pays me accordingly. I'm more than grateful for this situation. Most of my law school friends are miserable or struggling to work their way to the top, with terrible bosses who ride their asses all day and night. Not me. I've got a great job that I love.

I sarcastically reply, "So thrilled I made the cut."

"Just barely. How was the signing?"

"It was great, thanks for asking."

She clutches her chest. "I just finished your new release. Oh, Gemma, it's your best book yet. I cried, I laughed, I swooned." She gives me a cheeky smile. "Jackson also says thank you."

I let out a laugh. "I don't think you two need any help in that department."

Despite being around fifty, Darian and her husband are very...*active*. Even in her office sometimes. It's the source of many jokes around here, though we're all a little jealous of the passion they share.

Darian was widowed in her mid-forties. The other people in this office say she had a rough few years after her husband passed, but then she met Jackson and things took a turn for the better. I only know her with Jackson. He's madly in love with her. Fairytale love. I may have based a few book characters on the two of them. They're like a romance novel come to life. In fact, maybe I should write their story. It would be a great book.

She winks. "What are you working on today?"

"The Henley contracts."

Her face falls. "If you have to meet with him in person again, I want you to take someone with you."

"Yeah, yeah. It wasn't a big deal. You're an attractive woman, Darian. I'm sure clients have hit on you in the past. Sadly, this situation isn't news for women in the workplace."

"Hit on me? Yes. But John Henley was more than hitting on you. He was completely out of line, Gemma. Nothing about the situation is acceptable. I wish you'd let me fire him as a client."

She went nuts when I told her about John Henley's constant sexual innuendos. They were truly over the top. I have a dirty sense of humor and can handle a lot, but it wasn't the time or place, and it certainly wasn't innocent fun. He was pushing to see if I'd bite on any of it.

I shake my head. "I'd rather hit him where it hurts. His pocketbook. It's a lot of billable hours for us."

"I don't care about the money. I care about you. *Never* be alone with him. Am I understood?"

I nod. "Yes. I promise."

"Jackson may have thrown him a little elbow at a fundraiser last week. He made it clear to John that he doesn't do business with anyone who mistreats women. If that doesn't set him straight, I want you to tell me right away. Zero tolerance. I let you talk me into giving him one more chance. It's the only one."

Jackson is one of the biggest developers in all of Philly. People fall all over themselves to do business with him.

"Yes, ma'am. How's the fam?"

"Wonderful. Are you still planning to come to our house for Thanksgiving?"

"If you'll have me. I don't want to intrude."

"We're looking forward to it." She lets out a laugh. "You look more like my daughter than two of my three girls." She jokes, "Reagan demanded a DNA test when she met you."

People often mistake us for mother and daughter, and even sometimes assume Darian is my older sister. I take it all as a compliment.

I shake my head. "Marian Fairchild is most definitely my mother. There's no escaping it."

She gives me a knowing smile. She's met my mother.

I ask, "You're okay that Val and CJ are coming, right?" My two best friends are family-less for Thanksgiving this year too.

"The more, the merrier. Don't work too late, Gemma. Make sure you have some fun. You work too hard."

"Said no other boss, ever."

She lets out a laugh and repeats her often-stated mantra, "Happy employees are productive employees," before heading back to her office.

"Andrew, I'm heading out to lunch."

Our young, adorable front desk receptionist looks up at me. "Okay, mademoiselle. Where are you headed?"

"I'm meeting Taylor at Parc."

"Yummy. I was just there with my man. Enjoy."

I walk into the French-styled chic restaurant, Parc, and see my friend waving at me from her table. Taylor and I met in college and have been fairly close ever since. We went to law school together, but she chose to work for a big law firm in their family law department, and I chose a small corporate firm.

She's in a white pantsuit, and her long blonde hair is styled in a fashionable ponytail. I smile as I approach. "Wow, you look gorgeous. That suit is amazing."

She bats her eyelashes. "Thank you, and I know. I'm obsessed with this suit." With a big dose of pride, she boasts, "I was in court this morning and wanted to kick a little ass."

I gasp. "They're finally letting you go to court?"

She hands me a glass of my favorite white wine as her big brown eyes sparkle with happiness. "Yes. About damn time. Vicious Victor finally let me off the leash. I need to get back to the office to debrief him, so I ordered for us already. I hope you don't mind."

Her boss, Victor, has been working her like a dog for years, barely giving her any real responsibility.

"Not at all. You know what I like." I take a sip. "Yum. This is good. Tell me about your case."

"Just an ugly divorce, nothing crazy. People get so petty. My client is the wife, and she makes a lot more money than he does. He refuses to contribute anything toward the kids, even though he makes a comfortable living. And then he tells the kids that they can't do certain things they want to do because their mother won't pay for it."

I blow out a breath. "Ugh. What a dick. That's so depressing. Why can't people get it together for their kids?"

She takes a big gulp of her wine. "I know. It's jading me on love. I'm terrified of it. And Victor is always telling me to never get married. I should switch departments, but I've put in more than four years already. I feel like I'd be starting over."

"If you're unhappy, make a change."

She bites her lip. "Maybe. You hit the lottery with your boss. We're not all that lucky."

"I know. I'm very fortunate. She invited me to join her family for Thanksgiving."

"That's so nice. You know you're always welcome to come with me to my family in Boston."

"I appreciate the offer, but with my mother away and the office closed for a few days, it will give me some time to focus on my writing."

"Oh right. How was your book thingy?"

And that's what several of my friends and family call it. *Book thingy* or *sex books*. They don't understand why I decided to write, and I often feel judged. I try to explain that they're love stories, because, at the end of the day, I'm a hopeless romantic, but they only see the lascivious side of things, and I've stopped bothering to explain it to them.

Taylor is more supportive than most. Though not a romance reader, she always buys my books just because they're mine, and she gives them the wonderful five-star reviews that we indie authors crave, and I appreciate it. But she still doesn't get it. I answer questions when asked but don't otherwise bring it up anymore. I have my author friends to talk to about it.

"It was so much fun."

"Is it a bunch of women in lingerie walking around looking for sex books?"

I spit my drink in laughter. "Umm, no. No one is in lingerie. It's no different from any other convention. Think about the Atlantic City boat show we went to a few years ago. That was boats and boat-related product companies with their own booths selling their products. This was authors selling their books and meeting romance readers."

She shrugs. "Don't spoil the illusion. I imagine it as one big orgy."

I smile as I shake my head. "Okay, sure. It's one massive orgy with a bunch of hornballs groping each other."

She grins. "Thanks for indulging me. It's cool that you have this fun hobby. All I do is work. I fit in a date or two now and then, but I feel like all I do is try to please Victor."

"Any interesting dates lately?"

She gasps. "Holy shit. That reminds me. I've been dying to tell you about one I had a few days ago. You're going to want it for one of your books. It was a guy I met on Hinge, not Tinder."

That's code for it being an actual date, not just a booty call.

"The date was going well. I don't like to put out on a first date if I'm genuinely interested, but after dinner, we were sitting in his car talking when he leaned over to kiss me."

"Aww. That's sweet."

"Just wait. It gets good. So, my eyes are closed while we're kissing, and he starts moaning. Loudly. Way more than normal for a kiss. I opened my eyes and saw his dick in his hand. He was jerking off while we kissed. On a first date."

"He just took out his dick? You didn't touch him or anything?"

"Other than my hands on the back of his neck, no. He jerked off during our first kiss as if it's a totally normal thing to do."

"That's so weird. Where…umm…did it go? When he came."

She leans over and whispers, "All over my fucking arm."

I burst out laughing. "Oh my god. That's classic. I'm definitely using that in a book." I type a quick note in my phone to remind myself of this ridiculous story.

She smiles as she nods. "I thought you might."

"How did you leave things with him? *Hey, thanks for the arm of jizz. Text me later.*"

She giggles. "He just sent me a text when I was in court this morning about wanting to see me again…and some other dirty stuff."

She blushes, which is very unlike her. I think she's into this guy.

"Did you respond?"

"No, I'm not good with the dirty banter. I need your help. You're the sex author."

"What did his last text say?"

"That he wants to see me again and can't get my sexy body out of his mind."

"Do you want to see him again?"

She bites her lip. "I think so. The dick thing was weird, but before that things were going really well. We have a lot in common and the chemistry was there."

"Write back that you'll think about it, but you'll need to bring wipes this time."

She scrunches her face. "Eww. I don't know if I can say that."

"Do it. Trust me."

She reluctantly pulls out her phone and types away. It pings seconds later with a response.

I stare at her as she reads it with a big smile. "What did he write?"

She looks back up at me. "That he's sorry he did that, but he couldn't help himself. That I'm so hot he needed to come. He simply couldn't wait until he got home."

"Write back that it *was* hot. That's why you're still wearing it."

She giggles. "No way. I'm not writing that."

I nod toward her phone and lift my eyebrow.

She sighs. "Ugh. Fine. You're turning me into a ho." She sends the text.

Again, her phone pings right away with a response.

After seeing her attempt to bite back a smile, I look at her in question. "Well? What did he write?"

"That the comment was so hot that he's got his dick in his hand again."

I laugh. "Told ya so. I'm a dirty talk professional. I have a PhD in sordid thoughts and naughty words."

"Thanks for your help. I miss your dirty mind. I wish we went out for more than just a monthly lunch."

My face falls. She's right. "I know. I get so absorbed in my writing. Nights and weekends are the only time I get to do it. I watch football and basketball with Val and CJ, but I haven't otherwise been doing much. Let's make time in the near future to go out."

She reaches over and squeezes my hand. "I'd love that. Val and CJ monopolize all your free time."

"You could always hang with the three of us."

"Umm…no. The three of you have a weird relationship. I'd feel like a fifth wheel even though I'd technically be the fourth."

I get that. Most people feel that way when hanging out with me and my forever besties.

She continues, "I'll let my girls know you're up for going out. They'd love to see you."

Ugh. I adore Taylor, but her friends are a bit much for me at times. They're obsessed with finding rich men. These are girls who went to college to get their M.R.S., as in trying to become a wife instead of caring about a real degree. They're the kind of women who completely change who they are and are willing to drop everything because of the men they're dating. I hate women like that.

It's probably why I rarely hang out with them anymore. It's all about the manhunt. And they're so judgy about my writing. But I'm committed to being more social, so I halfheartedly agree.

I FINISH work and am at the bar a little early, waiting for Trey Donatucci to arrive. I speak into my phone, "Yes, Lubey Libby, I'm meeting with the plumber now."

She cheerfully asks, "What's a plumber's favorite casino game?"

"I don't know. What?"

"Craps."

I let out a laugh as I motion for the bartender to refill my vodka martini. I need a little more liquid courage for tonight. I have no idea what the hell I'm doing.

"That's a terrible joke. But also funny."

"This is so exciting, Gem. You're the first of us to meet with a BBB client. Do you know what kind of book boyfriend you want him to be? A sweet cinnamon roll type, or an alpha dirty man? *Roar.*"

"Did you just claw at me even though I can't see you?"

She giggles. "Yes. It's so thrilling that we get to mold men. Well? Which is it?"

"Hmm. I think I need to get to know him first. I don't want to make him into something he's not. Don't we simply want to help draw out the best in these guys? And teach them to better read women and their needs? I don't think we should be helping men dupe women."

I mouth, "Thank you," to the waiter as he refills my drink.

"So…you won't tell him to bend her over, spank her, and go straight to anal on the first date?"

I burst out laughing. "Oh my god. You're terrible. Maybe I'll just tell him the *real* secret to every woman's heart and pants. We all want men with pierced cocks." I sarcastically add, "I know I only sleep with men who have dick piercings. Everything else is bearable if they make us black out when we come."

She moans. "Umm. That sounds like heaven."

I moan too. "I know, and—"

My conversation is interrupted by a tap on the shoulder followed by a raspy, deep voice. "Excuse me."

I turn around and am completely dumbfounded. Before me is the most objectively attractive man I've ever seen in my life. He's tall and muscular, with dark hair and blue eyes. His face is full of sexy scruff, but it's the chin dimple that truly catches my attention. *Fuuuck.* Is Santa filling my stocking early this year?

I actually blink a few times, thinking I might be dreaming about the man staring at me. Am I being pranked right now? I don't see any cameras. Maybe my vibrator manifested this.

My mouth fills with saliva. I gulp it down before responding, "Can…can…I help you?"

He holds out his hand. "I'm Trey. Your…umm…*client.* I recognize you from your videos."

"*You're* Trey Donatucci? My new client?" There's no way.

He smiles sexily. "I am."

The slovenly middle-aged man sitting next to me at the bar clears his throat, loud enough to gain my attention. Looking my body up and down, he licks his lips and says, "Oh, I didn't realize you're one of *those* kinds of girls. Can I get an appointment after him? I'd like to be a *client* too." He air quotes the word *client.*

Before I can register the insult, Trey grabs the man by the shirt and pushes him against the bar. "This is a business meeting, asshole. Does she look like that type of woman?"

They both visibly take in my hunter-green designer Prada business suit. It's one of my most conservative outfits. I'm even wearing a red Hermes scarf around my neck. Short of wearing a bonnet, I couldn't possibly look any more conservative. There's certainly nothing about me to suggest *call girl.*

Trey glares back at the guy, bringing his face within an inch of the man's. He practically growls, yes growls, "Fucking apologize to her."

Nope, my panties aren't soaked right now.

The man, much smaller than Trey, looks scared to death. "I'm…I'm sorry, ma'am."

I can only wordlessly nod. I breathe into the phone, "Later, Lib."

She yells out, "No. I want to listen. That was so fucking h—"

I end the call and gain a little composure before glaring at the man at the bar. "Be careful how you speak to women and the assumptions you make. For example, I'm assuming right now that you're not very well endowed and potentially suffer from a little premature ejaculation issue. But perhaps I'm wrong."

I innocently smile and bat my eyelashes.

Trey lets out a laugh but hasn't let go of him yet. The man still looks terrified. Frankly, I don't care about the stranger or what he said. I'm focused on reining in the throb between my legs at this entire alpha display.

Realizing the situation needs to be defused, I quickly throw my bag over my shoulder, grab my drink, leave too much cash for the bartender, and slide off the stool. "Trey, let's get a table so we can talk. I think there's been some sort of misunderstanding between us."

He nods as he releases the man, who breathes a sigh of relief.

Trey follows me as I flag down the hostess and secure a table as far away from the bar as possible. Trey is so close behind me that I can smell his delicious aftershave. It's invading my senses. Who smells this good? What the hell is happening?

Wait. I think I just heard him inhale. Did he just smell me too?

We make our way to the back and sit across from one another at a small table. He exhales a deep breath while running his fingers through his hair. "I owe you an apology. He was being disrespectful to you, and I snapped. It's completely out of character for me to act like that. I'm not a violent person. I don't know what came over me. I'm sorry. I hope I didn't scare you."

I can't help the small twinge of disappointment that I experience. And then I'm surprised I feel that way. I've never witnessed a fight, let alone one over me. It wasn't really a fight. More like a strong man demoralizing a weak one. Well, I suppose I helped demoralize him too, but he was an asshole and deserved it.

I nonetheless force a smile. "It's okay. You were well-intended. Why don't we grab you a drink and start over?"

And I need a minute to figure out what he's doing here. I'm confused. This man doesn't need my services.

He nods. "Thank you. I'd like that."

He motions for the waitress, who appears immediately, which is not at all surprising for a guy like Trey. He orders a beer while I down a few large gulps of my vodka martini.

I take in his entire appearance. He's in jeans that hug what appear to be extremely muscular thighs. His black sweater does little to disguise his broad chest and muscles. His hair is thick and wavy. He's extremely tall. The whole package is perfection. He belongs on the cover of one of my books.

After he orders, he looks at me with his piercing blue eyes. "I'm going to assume your name isn't Tami Maida. What's your real name?"

I can't help but smile. "I've been writing for nearly three years. You're the first person to ever connect the dots on my pen name without me having to explain it to them."

He smirks. "I have a sister. She must have watched the movie *Quarterback Princess* a thousand times when we were kids. It's a classic. Did you know that it's loosely based on a true story?"

Quarterback Princess is a movie about a girl, Tami Maida, who leads her high school's football team as the star quarterback and is also the prom queen.

"Of course I do. I was the only girl on my high school's football team. I was the kicker though, not the quarterback. Though I did get to play quarterback for two plays at the end of the season." I mock blow my fingernails. "I don't mean to brag, but I do have one completion for eighteen yards on my resumé."

His eyes widen in shock. "Really? I wouldn't have guessed that about you."

"Why not?"

"Hmm. I'm not sure. You're kind of…girly."

I giggle. "They're not mutually exclusive. You can be both."

He humbly nods, knowing he's been busted for judging this book by its cover. "I suppose you can. Lesson learned, though

I'm going to assume you were also the prom queen. I know I'm not wrong about that one."

The corners of my mouth raise in amusement. "I was. And my real name is Gemma Fairchild. I'm an attorney."

He pinches his thick eyebrows together. "I thought that you're an author?"

"Being an author doesn't pay the bills. In fact, it adds to them. It's more of a labor of love. A hobby." I hold out my hand to shake his. "It's nice to meet you, Trey Donatucci."

He flinches for a brief moment before taking my hand in his enormous and calloused one. It occurs to me that I've never been touched by a man with calloused hands. It's unexpectedly appealing and sexy as hell.

He continues to hold my hand in his. "That's a pretty name for a pretty lady."

I smile as I slowly, and begrudgingly, pull my hand away. "Thank you, but aren't *I* supposed to be the one teaching *you* how to flirt properly? You seem pretty good at it already."

He gives me a boyish grin before he rubs his scruff with his fingers. "I suppose you're right." He makes a show of zipping his lips and throwing away the imaginary key. "Pretend I'm a blank canvas. Teach me, Master Gemma."

I laugh as I pull out my notebook and pen, suddenly intrigued by this whole bizarre situation. "Why don't we get to business? I read your application and know a little background from it…but tell me why a man like you reached out to me."

His eyes are playful. "I think I wrote that on my application."

"You did, and it was very clever. It certainly caught my eye. But what's the real reason? You're a…good-looking guy, Trey. I'm sure you don't have trouble finding women."

"I don't want any woman. I want the right one."

"What does the right one look like?"

He contemplates for a moment before answering, "One who doesn't judge me for my job."

"Your job?" That's interesting. "Being a plumber is a noble profession. But I've never had a plumber who looks like you."

He looks like a porn plumber where the dirty housewife has her wicked way with him while he's on his back, working under her kitchen sink.

Damn it. I need to stop watching so much porn.

He briefly looks away. I know that means he's not being truthful. He's searching for a lie right now.

Leaning back, I say, "This doesn't work if you're not honest with me. In the words of Thomas Jefferson, *honesty is the first chapter in the book of wisdom.* It's a trait I value above all others."

"I've never had a date quote Thomas Jefferson before."

"This isn't a date. It's a business meeting."

He holds his hands up. "You're right. I'm sorry. This is as new to me as it is to you. It's hard for me to articulate the right woman. I'm still figuring it out myself."

"Fair enough, but this isn't a matchmaking service. I want to make sure you realize that. I need you to be here for the right reasons, Trey."

"My intentions are noble, I assure you. I'm just looking to understand you better."

"Understand who better?"

He quickly corrects himself. "Women. I'm looking to understand women better. I saw your video, and everything about it was appealing to me. I'm here to learn from the expert."

I hold up my left hand and wiggle my ringless ring finger. "I'm hardly an expert. I barely even date. My doctor asked me last week if there's any chance that I'm pregnant. I responded that if I am, I'd be giving birth to batteries."

He lets out a loud laugh. "Right, you're a rom-com author. You're funny."

I smile. "I try. But in all seriousness, all I'm offering is to show you what women find so appealing about book boyfriends. There's no magic formula. It's up to you to decide which of those attributes makes sense for you. I'm not encouraging you to act in a way inconsistent with your own personality. We want an enhanced and enlightened Trey, not a deceitful Trey. Does that make sense?"

He nods. "I understand. How do we get started?"

"Tell me a little about yourself."

He blows out a breath. "Well, I'm twenty-nine. I enjoy sports, especially football, and my job. I have an older sister who I'm close to, a niece who's my favorite person in the world, and a baby nephew who's just finding his voice. My parents divorced when we were teens. My sister and I relied on each other a lot."

I nod in understanding. "Mine divorced when I was a teen too. It's no walk in the park. You're lucky you had a sister to rely on. It can be very lonely."

"No siblings?"

I shake my head. "No, but I'm close with my grandmother. I spent a lot of time with her when I needed a break from the madness. Where do you live, Trey?"

"Umm, in the city."

"Do you have many friends?"

He smiles. It's the most genuine one he's given me yet, and it's adorable. "I do. I have a great group of friends. Most of them are still single too. We have fun together."

"What's your definition of fun?"

"Like I said, sports. Mostly hanging out with my crew. Going to clubs and bars. Nothing extraordinary. I travel a little when I can, but I'm just a normal twenty-nine-year-old guy."

"I understand."

I'm still unclear why a man like him needs help, but I decide to stay the course and see how this plays out. "Let's talk book boyfriends. We're cracking the code on what fictitious men have that real men don't. For today, I just planned to get to know you a little bit and then educate you on some romance novel terminology. Are you familiar with the word *trope*?"

"No. Should I be?"

"Not necessarily. I didn't know it before I started writing. It's a common theme that you see in a given book. An overarching concept. Romance books are known for having them. At some point, there were probably only a dozen or so, but it's taken on a life of its own, and now there are hundreds. Romance readers are attracted to different tropes depending on their personalities, wants, and needs."

He twists his lips. "I'm not following. Can you give me an example?"

"Sure. A very popular trope is enemies to lovers, where the couple starts off hating each other, and then that hateful passion morphs throughout the book into steamy, bedroom passion. It's usually followed by a happily ever after."

He scrunches his face. "I can't imagine hating a woman and then magically falling in love with her. That's weird."

"Frankly, I feel the same. I've only written one book with that trope, and, between you and me, they weren't true enemies. More like business competitors."

He nods. "I can see *that* being hot. What are other examples of tropes?"

"Friends to lovers, billionaire, second chance, fake relationships, forbidden—"

"Forbidden? What does that mean?"

I shrug. "A bunch of different things. Sometimes it might be teacher/student or employer/employee, but it's probably most often used in romances between stepsiblings or a stepdaughter and her stepfather."

He makes a look of disgust. "Do you write those?"

I shake my head. "I don't, but I respect those who do. I've read some, I just don't write them. I keep things fairly light-hearted. I write the kind of men I'd like to date, and I'm okay with the fact that it may not be for everyone."

"What does all this mean for me and your service? Do I have to pick a trope and become that guy?"

I let out a laugh. "No, not at all. I'm just creating awareness of all the different types of themes in these romance novels.

Each woman is attracted to something different. For example, some like what is termed a cinnamon roll or golden retriever man."

"What are those?"

"Sweet, supportive, kind book boyfriends."

"All women don't want that?"

"No, they don't. Some want alpha or possessive men. Men who practically growl. Many women like that *touch her and die* vibe. Or the *who hurt you* vibe."

His eyes meet mine. "Which kind do you like, Gemma?"

I feel my cheeks redden. "In all honesty, I think I'd like a bit of both. There are times for sweet and supportive and times I want a man who takes a little control and will fight for me."

"Have you ever found one who is both? The whole package?"

Shaking my head, I admit, "I haven't. Maybe he doesn't exist."

He calmly leans back in his chair. "Maybe you've been looking in the wrong places."

Maybe he's right.

We're both silent for a few long beats as we sip our drinks.

Eventually, he asks, "What are other tropes?"

"There are hundreds of them. I swear, I see new ones pop up every single day. We could talk about tropes for hours. There are fake marriages, surprise pregnancies, secret babies, mistaken identity, forced proximity, age gaps, bodyguards, shared bed, kidnappers, stalkers, sports—"

He perks up at that. "There are sports romances?"

I nod. "Lots of them. Women get off on jocks."

"Do *you* get off on jocks?"

I sigh. "We're not here to talk about me. This isn't a date." *Though I wouldn't mind if it was.* "I'm here to help you better understand women's desires and needs."

He takes another sip of his beer. It's almost erotic how sexy it is when he swallows. His Adam's apple slides up and then back down. He exudes confidence with his legs spread wide. He's so…manly.

He licks the beer off his lower lip. "I think it would be helpful for me to get firsthand information. Obviously you're not married. Are you seeing anyone?"

I shake my head. "Not currently."

"Why didn't it work out with your last boyfriend?"

I grimace.

His face falls. "I'm sorry. I didn't mean to pry."

"Yes, you did, but it's fine. Frankly, he wasn't either a cinnamon roll or a possessive man." I've never thought of it that way, but it's true. "The biggest problem was that he wasn't… supportive."

"In what ways?"

"I'm a lawyer, and he works in finance. I think, on paper, we made a lot of sense, both being what we each thought we wanted in a partner. He didn't love how brash I can be, and he struggled with my romance writing career. He was embarrassed by it. Embarrassed by me."

Trey waves his hand dismissively. "Fuck him. I think it's cool that you write books."

"Thank you. It was more than just that. He didn't give me…that something extra. He accused me of thinking the men in my books were real. And that's, in part, why we started this business. We're trying to help men figure out how to play into the fantasies of women. The small things that go a long way."

"What was his trope?"

I smile. "Ooh, that's a tough one. As I've spent the past few months thinking about it, I think he was the asshole ex that is often present in romance books. The one the female character didn't realize was Mr. Wrong until after they broke up but feels like a fool for not seeing it earlier until she realizes it was part of the journey to finding Mr. Right." I mumble, "At least I hope I'm on that journey."

He nods in understanding. "I've had a few Ms. Wrongs in my past too. How do I become the kind of boyfriend you want?"

"Different women want different things. Romance readers get fully engrossed in novels. They don't slowly read our books. They don't read a chapter a night for several weeks. They binge. Some read five or six books a week. Why do you think that is?"

He shrugs. "The sex scenes?"

I let out a laugh. "Maybe a little of that, but no, I don't think that's it. There are generally only five or six sex scenes in a full-length book. They're a tiny percentage of the overall story. What they enjoy is the fantasy. A man who feeds into the dialogue of something they're missing, something they want, or simply something that merely excites them."

"Give me an example."

I think for a moment. How can I best make this relatable to him? An idea occurs to me. "How about grand romantic gestures? Something huge and thoughtful that fictional men often do for their women. I know you don't read romance novels, but have you seen romantic comedy movies?"

"Of course."

"Isn't there always some grand romantic gesture at the end of those movies? Richard Gere rides in with his head sticking out of his limo and climbs the fire escape for her in *Pretty Woman,* giving her the fairytale she once mentioned wanting. Harry runs through the entire city of New York on New Year's Eve and interrupts a fancy party just to tell Sally he wants to spend his life with her in *When Harry Met Sally.* Nick boarded a plane and dropped down to one knee in front of everyone with his mother's emerald ring in *Crazy Rich Asians.* In *Hitch,* he freakin' jumps on top of a moving car at the end to spill his heart out to her."

Trey nods. "I get it." He whispers, more to himself than me, "Grand romantic gestures."

"There are thousands of things like that. Something that makes a woman's heart beat faster. Something that makes her feel seen, important, and cared for. In all honesty, Trey, what you did at the bar is something you might read in a romance novel and not see as much in real life."

"What do you mean?"

"You got *very* protective of me. A lot of women would get off on that. Frankly, it was hot. I might write about it."

He smirks with pride. "Really?" He mock straightens his shirt and holds his shoulders high. "I think I'm already learning to be a good book boyfriend just by being around you."

I giggle. "Yes, you are."

"By the way, *Crazy Rich Asians* is one of the funniest movies I've seen in a long time."

I smile. "Agree. Did you know that it was a rom-com book first?"

"No, I didn't. That's cool. Will your books be movies?"

I let out a loud laugh. "I wish. That's the dream of almost every author but the reality for very few."

"Dream big, Gemma. That's why I'm here. Nothing will stand in the way of me getting the woman I want."

I swallow. "I'm sensing you have a particular woman in mind."

He smiles. "I suppose you're right."

"What's her name?"

For the first time, he looks a little flustered. Maybe he doesn't want me to know.

"Umm…Jenna."

"Okay. Tell me about Jenna."

He has a dreamy look on his face. "She's the most beautiful woman I've ever seen in my life. The second I laid eyes on her, I knew I wanted her to be mine. I can't explain it. Her laugh. Her smile. She's…she's extraordinary. There's something about her that immediately struck a chord in me. I've never felt that way about a woman before."

"In the romance world, we call that insta-love."

"Like love at first sight?"

"Yes. It's another trope. Tell me about your interactions with her."

"I've only spoken to her once, but I *really* like what I've seen."

"Why only once?"

"I don't want to mess it up. I also only recently met her."

"Does she know how you feel?"

He shakes his head. "No. I don't want to scare her off."

I slowly nod. "I guess it would be a risk. Some women might be into insta-love, but some might be frightened off by you coming on that strong."

"That's what I was thinking. I need to be careful so I don't screw it up."

"What does she know about you?"

"Pretty much everything I've told you."

"What do you know about her?"

He bites back a smile. He's clearly besotted with this lucky woman. I have a pang of jealousy over her.

"Besides being stunning, she's funny, super smart, and kind of…uptown."

"Do you have any clue as to what she's looking for in a man?"

"I'm learning. Tell me some more things that romance readers like *you* want in a book boyfriend. Better yet, tell me things you don't. That could be helpful in getting to…generally know women's wants and needs."

I twist my lips for a moment. "I think many women are attracted to book boyfriends who only have eyes for them. All others be damned. Men who love the female lead character and don't care who knows it."

"Like a public display of affection?"

"It's more than that. It's about unashamedly loving them. My ex didn't like to kiss in public. He said it was because of my red lipstick. For some reason, that always bothered me. If a man loves you, why would he care about a little lipstick on his face?

Shouldn't he value kissing you over any small embarrassment that might cause?"

Trey nods as he stares at my lips. "I'd wear it proudly."

We're silent as he continues to stare.

What's happening? Is it getting hot in here?

It's time to end this. "I've given you a lot to consider. Why don't you think about some of these things, and we can meet after you've had time to process them? Perhaps you can learn a bit more about Jenna and her needs. Like I said, I'm not here to play matchmaker, but I do want to bring out the best version of you."

It's actually sweet that he's so besotted and wants to learn how to make this woman happy. Perhaps our arrangement will work out after all.

He nods. "I'd like that. I'll reach out soon."

CHAPTER

Four

TREY

AS I WALK BACK to Layton's penthouse, I think about Gemma. She's even more incredible than I imagined. She's the full package. Sexy, smart, funny. Everything. *Did I mention sexy?* Even her conservative outfit couldn't mask those curves.

I think I have exactly what she mentioned. *Insta-love*. It took every ounce of restraint in my body not to lean across the table, grab her gorgeous face, and kiss her. Her sultry, red-painted lips will be playing in my fantasies tonight. I'd kill to have that lipstick on my face.

I can't mess this up. I want to learn everything about her and everything she needs before I make my move.

The one thing I know for sure is that I have to read all her books to understand the kind of men she likes. I quickly pull up my phone and type in her pen name. She's written six books. Wow. I order them all on Amazon. They'll be delivered to Layton's place by tomorrow.

I'm staying there indefinitely. I have nearly four months until spring training in Florida starts. Layton has a ton of space and doesn't care how long I live with him. He's stayed with me in New York countless times.

About twenty minutes later, I walk into Layton's enormous condo. He and Cheetah are sitting on the couch playing a video game. Without taking his eyes off the television, Cheetah asks, "How did it go? Are you a real-life Casanova now? Did you win the damsel in distress? Did you diddle the duchess? Did you bang the belle of Broad Street?"

I plop down on a chair next to them and sigh dreamily. "She's perfect. I have insta-love."

Cheetah chuckles while Layton appears confused. "What's that?"

Cheetah answers, "A romance book trope. It's short for instant love. You also have a case of the *he falls first* trope."

I question, "What's that?"

"Exactly what it sounds like. When the guy falls before the woman. Hard."

I nod. "I definitely have a case of *he falls first*. She's so fucking beautiful. Her lips and green eyes will be in my dreams tonight. The thickest natural lips I've ever seen."

Cheetah does his best deep, big bad wolf voice, and bellows, "Moowahahaha. All the better to suck your dick with, my dear."

I chuckle. "Something like that. Speaking of dicks, I need your help with something."

Layton raises an eyebrow. "There will be no dick sucking. I'm letting you stay here indefinitely until you rope her in, but I have my friendship limits."

I roll my eyes. "Not that, asshole. I think I want to get my dick pierced."

Cheetah gives a knowing smile. "Chicks in romance novels love that. Half the books now have men with piercings."

"Yep. I think real women like them too. Gemma does."

"She told you that?" Layton asks. "It seems like a weird topic for a first date."

"It wasn't a date, and no, she didn't tell me, but I heard her on the phone with her friend. She said all women like men with pierced cocks, especially her."

Layton shakes his head. "I can't believe you're willing to put extra holes in your dick for this woman. You just met her an hour ago."

"She's the one. I have zero doubts. I'll do whatever it takes. She said women like grand romantic gestures. This will be my first for her. The first of many."

The two of them laugh, thinking that I'm joking, but I'm not. Gemma Fairchild is the perfect woman, and I want her as mine. I'm willing to do whatever it takes.

I take a deep breath and nod my head toward his bar area. "I need whiskey before we go. There's no way I can do this sober."

After downing about half a bottle of whiskey and feeling very numb, we make our way to the dick-piercing store down on South Street. Layton and Cheetah downed the other half of the bottle, claiming that they couldn't watch this sober.

We sit in the lobby area while browsing the piercing store's brochure. I had no clue that there were so many options when it comes to getting your dick pierced.

We're waiting there for at least twenty minutes. My nerves are starting to get the best of me, but I'm determined to see this through.

Cheetah remarks, "I read one of her books. The guy talks dirty. Like, *really* dirty. Maybe she's into that."

"She said she writes about the kind of men she likes. I ordered all her books. I think it will be a good way to get to know what she's into."

Cheetah scoffs. "I've been telling you guys for years that romance novels are like instruction manuals for women. You never listen."

"I never needed to…until now."

We're interrupted by a woman with a nasally voice shouting from one of the piercing rooms, "Next."

I wipe my sweaty palms on my jeans as the three of us walk back into the room. It looks like a makeshift doctor's office with an examination table. My knees are literally shaking. The woman has pink hair, black lipstick, and a thousand piercings all over her body. I can't believe I'm about to let this woman poke a hole in my dick.

I close my eyes and think about what Gemma looked like walking to the table. Her sexy body. The way she smelled. The way she made me laugh. And I love how smart she is. Perfection.

I open my eyes feeling resolute. This is for Gemma.

The piercing woman chews her gum loudly as her eyes move up and down my body. She gives me an unimpressed look. In a Philly accent, she asks, "First time?"

I nod.

"Prince Albert, I assume?"

I nod again. "It seems like it's the best one to get."

She nonchalantly shrugs. "I suppose it's a good gateway drug. It will wet yas appetite." She winks. "Pun intended."

"And it's pleasurable for the woman, right?"

She pops her gum and smiles. "Ya bet, stud."

Cheetah asks, "What about the man? Is it pleasurable or painful for him?"

One corner of her mouth raises. "After it heals, yas will have the best orgasms of yas life. Money-back guarantee. And once it's healed, yas can take it in and out freely. It's easy."

That makes sense to me. Playing baseball with jewelry in my dick could be problematic. It's good that I can take it out for games. I cringe at the notion of sliding headfirst and anything…catching. Pulling. Tearing. I get the shivers thinking about it.

I take a few deep breaths, feeling like I might pass out.

This is for Gemma. This is for Gemma.

I keep repeating it in my head. I think of her gorgeous face. How much I want to please her. Fuck, how am I already so far gone for this woman? I just met her.

And then I think of her big lips wrapped around the piercing. Oh shit, that would be hot.

Stop. I don't need a chub in here.

Layton slaps my back, bringing me back to reality. "It's not too late. You can back out."

"No. I'm doing this." I look back at her. "What's the recovery time?"

Her head toggles from shoulder to shoulder as she contemplates it. "Ahh...few weeks. It's not bad. It's probably the quickest recovery time of all the cock piercings. Are yas ready? I got lots of willing participants in the waiting area."

I nod. "Yes. Let's do it."

"Ya pay first. Ya know, just in case ya pass out or change ya mind. No refunds."

I take care of the payment, leaving a hefty tip to incentivize her to take extra-good care of me.

The woman commands, "Drop ya pants and get up on the table."

I do as she instructs. Cheetah looks at her. "I understand you're supposed to be hard for this. Can you lick around the tip a little for him?"

He chuckles and the woman simply pops her gum again like she's heard it all a thousand times before. She undoubtedly has.

He then gets uncomfortably close to me. I hold up my hand. "Dude, step back. I don't need you in my junk."

He continues staring. "You've got a big dick, DePaul. Mazel Tov. The head isn't as big as Layton's, but it's big. Lancaster's dick looks like a hammerhead shark."

I narrow my eyes at him. "Why do you know that?"

"We're teammates. We share a locker room," he mumbles, "and sometimes women."

I turn to Layton, and he nods. "I do have an unusually big head. Cheetah has huge balls though. Like bizarrely big."

I look at them both with disgust. "Your team is fucking weird. I'm glad I play for the Bombers and not the Cougars. We don't sit in the locker room and stare at each other's dicks all day."

The woman snickers. I'm thrilled we're amusing her.

She cleans all around my tip and then starts to move the needle toward me. I grit out, "Oh fuck. Oh fuck. Oh fuck."

Layton grabs my hand, but as soon as the needle makes contact with my tip, his eyes roll to the back of his head and he crumbles to the ground, passing out cold.

The woman turns her head toward the door and shouts, "Gunnar, we need the salt. Again."

A big, leather-clad, bald guy with even more piercings than her walks in and bends before running something under Layton's nose until he wakes up.

He blinks his eyes a few times. "Shit. That was intense. Is it over?"

I shake my head. "It didn't start. You're such a pussy. It's not even your dick." I lift my head and look at the woman. "He's fine. Go ahead."

The needle touches my tip again and…Cheetah passes out. I throw my hands in the air. "Are you guys kidding me? I'm the one whose dick is getting stuck with a needle."

After the behemoth repeats the same routine with Cheetah, I finally get the piercing. It's potentially the worst pain I've ever known in my life, and I bleed like a stuck pig, but I have an endgame in mind and nothing will deter me.

CHAPTER
Five

IT'S AN UNUSUALLY mild Saturday for this time of year. Gemma suggested we have coffee while we go for a walk. We agree to meet at a specific location on Broad Street, a historic city street.

I'm wearing a non-Bombers baseball cap and aviator sunglasses. I'm not usually recognized in Philly like I am in New York, but better safe than sorry.

I'm also wearing loose-fitting gray sweatpants. It's been a few days since I got the piercing, and I seem to be healing, but being around her will be tough. I'm terrified that I'll get hard and it will pull something.

I notice her sitting on a bench right away. She's dressed a bit more casually today, though she still looks amazing. She's in tight jeans, boots, and some sort of stylish sweater with an equally stylish scarf. Her oversized sunglasses give her a mysterious, sexy vibe.

Who am I kidding? Everything about her is sexy.

She waves and smiles as I approach. So fucking beautiful.

Without thinking, I bend to kiss her cheek and inhale her scent. "You look pretty. You smell nice too."

She sucks in a breath. I clearly caught her off guard.

"Sorry. Umm...here's your coffee with a splash of skim milk, per your request." I hand it to her, practically shoving it into her hands.

She tentatively takes it from me. "Thank you. It was sweet of you to offer to buy it on your way."

"My pleasure."

She stands and lifts her purse strap so it's running across her chest, and then links her arm through mine. "Let's walk and talk while we drink our coffees."

"Sounds good."

Normally I'd be ecstatic that she's touching me, but I can't get hard.

Smelly locker rooms. Smelly locker rooms.

I seem okay, so I smile down at her. "Did you have a nice week?"

"I did, thank you." She audibly exhales. "I was thinking about our conversation from the other night. I feel like I threw you into the deep end. We should take a step back and talk about some of the smaller things that book boyfriends do to make women happy."

"Like what?"

"Well..." She looks down at our linked arms. "This. Subtle touching. Locked arms, holding hands, lower back touches, neck or arm touches, and basically any contact that's not traditionally sexual. Book boyfriends often find it hard to keep their hands off their women. They want to be in her airspace at all times."

I understand the feeling.

"Are those things you like?"

She thinks for a moment. "I think I would, with the right person. With the wrong person, I can imagine it would be a little suffocating."

I think back to the two books of hers I read this week. There's definitely a lot of touching. And she always has the men grabbing the women by the hips.

Incidentally, reading her books while my dick is healing was a mistake. In every fictitious sexual encounter, I was imagining her and me. My piercing kept pulling. I earmarked the sex scenes and will come back to them in another week or two.

"What about hips? I'm a hip man. I love touching the curve of a woman's hip."

I can't help but look down at where her jeans hug her shapely hips perfectly. She's effortlessly sensuous.

She swallows. "Absolutely. Hip grabbing is good. *Very* good. Have you spoken with Jenna at all?"

I nod. "I have. I'm learning more about her every day."

She smiles, though it doesn't quite reach her eyes. "That's great. Are you going to see her again?"

"Yes, today."

"Wonderful. Make sure you're engaged with her. Listen to her and respond accordingly. Don't just nod your head. Ask follow-up questions. Men who talk about themselves throughout an entire date are red flags. They're narcissists. Dating is about equally getting to know each other, right? Book boyfriends hang on every word from the object of their affection and respond accordingly."

"Of course. What was your best first date?"

"Ooh. Tough one. It's been a while since I've had a good first date."

I see the moment it hits her. A small smile finds her full lips.

"I know this sounds cheesy, but when I was fifteen, I went on a date with a boy a year older than me. He drove, which was a big deal at the time. He picked me up at my house and opened the passenger's side car door for me. When I looked inside, there was a single red rose sitting on the seat waiting for me. It was just the sweetest, most thoughtful moment, and it set the tone for a nice evening."

"You like flowers?"

"Well, I suppose, but it was the thoughtfulness that struck a chord, not the flower per se. The fact that he considered me earlier in the day enough to buy me a flower was special. Women want to feel special. Book boyfriends think about their women before the date and do considerate things like that. It doesn't have to be excessive or expensive. Just small gestures like that, letting her know she was on his mind. Asking me how I take my coffee so you can buy me a cup is a great example of that."

"I understand. What are some other good book-boyfriend first-date gestures?"

"Hmm. Let me think about what a book boyfriend would do that most men don't do in real life. Oh, I've got one. On a normal dinner date, you sit across from the person, right?"

"Yes."

"In romance novels, the men always want to be as close to their woman as possible. They sit on the same side of the booth. It enables more physical intimacy."

I wordlessly nod, absorbing what she's saying when her phone rings. She pulls it out and looks at it. "Sorry. It's my mother. Do you mind if I take it? She doesn't usually call for no reason. She's not a chit-chat person."

"Go ahead."

She answers on speaker. "Hi, Mom. I'm in a meeting. Is everything okay?"

Her mother answers. "It's Saturday, Gemma. Why are you in a meeting? You work too much. You'll never find yourself a husband if you work this hard."

Gemma rolls her eyes. "Thank you for your unsolicited opinion. Is there something you *need*?"

"Yes. Byron is having a poolside luncheon two weeks from

today, and I want you to come. His daughter is in town, and I'd like you to meet her."

"A poolside luncheon? It's nearly winter."

"He has an indoor pool in addition to the outdoor one. The house is truly stunning. It was featured in *Architectural Digest* last year. You'll love it."

I see that her coffee is empty and feel like I should give her some privacy. I lean over and quietly ask, "Do you want a refill?"

Before she can answer, her mother asks, "Is that a man's voice? Are you on a date?"

"No, he's just a friend."

Her phone pings that her mother is now changing the audio call to a video call. Gemma sighs as she answers. She gives a clearly fake smile. "Hello, Mother."

"Turn the phone to your date."

"He's not my date. He's a friend."

She commands, "Turn the phone."

Gemma turns the screen toward me. Her mom is an attractive woman. She has Gemma's coloring, hair, and facial features but not her gorgeous green eyes. She must have gotten them from her father.

I smile. "Hello, Mrs. Fairchild."

"Well hello to you too, mister tall, dark, and handsome. What's your name?"

Gemma covers her eyes in mortification. It's adorable.

"Trey."

"Well, Trey, please join Gemma as her date for the gathering. I'd love to meet you."

Gemma grabs the phone. "Trey is busy. He can't come."

I hear her mom's voice. "Is that true, Trey?"

I mouth to Gemma. "It's not a big deal." So her mom can hear me, I answer, "I can move some things around. I'd love to come."

"Wonderful. I'll text Gemma the details. I'm thrilled that Gemma *finally* has a boyfriend."

"Mom, he's not my—"

Before Gemma can correct her again, her mom hangs up. She blows out a breath. "I'm so sorry about that. I'll make up an excuse as to why you can't come. I can't imagine going to her boyfriend's house is at the top of your to-do list."

I shrug. "It's not a big deal. I'm happy to go. I have nothing else going on that day."

An idea occurs to me. "Maybe I can practice my book-boyfriend moves on you. You can tell me if I'm doing them right and give me some...on-the-job training. It will be like a trial run."

She runs her bottom lip through her teeth.

Smelly locker rooms. Smelly locker rooms.

"I suppose that could work, and I wouldn't mind the familiar face. I want to prepare you. My mom is kind of a snob, and her life's mission is for me to get married and have kids. She'll probably have an officiant at her boyfriend's house to marry us."

I let out a laugh. "My mom too. It's fine."

"Thank you. It's very kind of you."

"I'm guessing this is a newer boyfriend since you haven't met his daughter yet?"

She nods. "Yes. I've only met him once, and my mother is a handful. She and I don't always see eye to eye on things."

"You mentioned a grandmother who helped you through the divorce. Is she still with us?"

She smiles. "Yes. She lives down on the west coast of Florida. I talk to her at least once a week. I'll be down there for Christmas. I know it's strange, but I love spending time with her and her friends. They're a riot. It gives me a little perspective. If that makes sense."

"It does. My niece does the same for me. I don't see her as

much as I'd like with my crazy schedule, but spending time with her, or even a phone call from her, is my happy place."

"Remind me, how old is she?"

"Four."

"Right. Where does your sister live?"

"In Greenwich, Connecticut. It's a great area."

Just then, a football lands at our feet and Gemma picks it up. We see kids down the block waving for us to throw it to them.

I hold out my hand. "It's a far throw. Do you want me to do it?"

She narrows her eyes at me. "No, Trey, I don't. I told you that I played football."

I can't help but smile at her indignation and decide to poke the bear a little more. "Weren't you a kicker? Are you going to kick it across the street?"

She hands me her coffee cup. "Hold my beer, big shot."

She rears back and rifles a perfect spiral right into the chest of a shocked teenage boy. If I wasn't in love already, I would be now.

I lift the corner of my mouth. "Well, I don't think I could have thrown it that well, quarterback princess."

She gives me a strong nod. "Damn right, you couldn't. That was Vance McCaffrey good."

I chuckle at her reference to the quarterback of Philadelphia's professional football team. "Do you watch football too?"

"Hell yes. I'm a football girl through and through. I bleed Philly green. I watch every game with my two best friends. What about you?"

I don't actually care for Philly football, but I don't think she'll like that answer. I keep it vague. "I love watching football. I go to some games now and then."

"Phew. I'd have to fire you as a client if you answered differently."

As we pass a coffee shop, I run inside to refill our cups before returning. We walk and talk a bit more until we approach City Hall. She looks up at the big Christmas tree with a smile.

I'm about to mention that I didn't know Philly had such a big Christmas tree on display when I catch myself. I suppose I should know that.

Instead, I ask, "Fond memories?"

She nods. "I grew up in the suburbs. My grandparents used to bring me down here at Christmas time to see the tree. My friends would go to New York to see the big one at Rockefeller Center, but my grandparents preferred this one. It's grown at a farm in Pennsylvania, and they were born and bred here. After my grandfather passed, my grandmother continued bringing me here every year until she moved to Florida."

We stare for a bit before sitting down on a bench. She looks at me. "Let's get back to book-boyfriend stuff. I know that's why you're here. I was talking to one of my author friends, and she felt like we'd be remiss not to talk about the big elephant in the room."

Oh shit. She knows.

I swallow. "What's that?"

"Sex. Sex in romance novels is very different from real-life sex. Novels tend to romanticize it a bit, setting women's expectations unfairly high."

"Maybe you've been having sex with the wrong men."

She brings her lips together, trying to fight a smile. "That was a good comeback. Nonetheless, it's true. Women don't come as easily and often as they do in romance novels."

I look her in the eyes. "Once again, perhaps you've been having sex with the wrong men."

She playfully narrows her eyes at me. "Okay, tough guy, I'm going to test you."

I smile. "Fire away."

"What does it mean when she screams that she's close?"

"That she's not seconds away, more like a minute or two."

"And what should you do?"

"Not change my pace or positioning."

She lifts an eyebrow. "Very good. A lot of men decide *that's* the time to change things up. Big mistake."

I wink. "What other sexual advice do you have for us unworthy non-book-boyfriends?"

"Dirty talk."

"What about it?"

"Every, and I mean *every*, woman likes it. They may vary in how dirty they like it, and how much of it they want, but no one likes a silent partner in bed. Most men struggle with it. Every man should read romance novels to learn how women want to be spoken to during sex."

"Noted. I promise to do some homework."

She has no idea what she's in store for.

CHAPTER

GEMMA

IT'S SATURDAY, and I'm getting ready to head to my mother's boyfriend's house with Trey pretending to be my boyfriend. I'm not sure how this happened.

I offered to pick Trey up to drive to the suburbs, but he said he'd meet me at my place.

We texted a handful of times throughout the past two weeks and met two more times for drinks. He's certainly taking this seriously, asking a ton of questions about book boyfriends and their tendencies.

As I pack two towels into my bag, my phone pings with a text notification. I see that it's my text group titled *Perverts*. That means it's my author friends.

> JoJo: Quick, I need something that could have only been invented by a man, besides individual coffee pods. Those are offensive.

> Libby: Metal toilet seats. Those are the devil's work.

Ava: LOL. True. I had to use one at my nephew's soccer game. My ass hasn't been the same since. I can tell you firsthand that the iFart app is the dumbest invention and clearly a man must have invented it. My ex-husband thought fart noises were hysterical.

Me: Crotchless panties. Only a man would think those are a good idea.

JoJo: True. So uncomfortable.

Libby: What about pet rocks? How dumb do you have to be? It had to be a man.

Me: We're missing the most obvious answer. High heels.

JoJo: Ooh. Good one. I'll use that. Thx!

We always text each other when we need something for a book and the answer isn't coming to our minds. I love how much we help each other.

Trey knocks on the door to my walkup brownstone at the agreed-upon time. Despite the chilly fall weather, he's in bathing suit bottoms and a Philadelphia football hoodie with aviator sunglasses. His legs, which I'm seeing for the first time, are extremely thick and muscular.

Maybe I'm used to more uptight men, but there's something different about Trey's masculinity and confidence, which I find very attractive. Jenna is a lucky woman.

He smiles as I open the door. "This place is great."

"Thank you. I bought it two years ago. I love the location."

It's right in the heart of Center City. I'm near all the shops and a few parks. Earning enough money to pay for a place like this is a tremendous source of pride for me.

He hands me a cup of coffee. "With a splash of skim milk, just as you like it."

I've known him for three weeks, and he knows how I take my coffee. I dated Aiden for two years and he never knew. Unreal.

"Thank you." I grab my cup and wave for him to enter. "Come in. I need to grab my bag."

He walks in and looks around before letting out a whistle. "Wow. You have amazing taste. I suppose it's not surprising, given how you dress, but this is gorgeous."

"It's my sanctuary. I guess I have an eye for interior decoration. I enjoy it."

"More than an eye. I feel like I'm walking into a magazine. Truly, it's one of the nicest places I've ever seen. Maybe I'm used to twenty-something, single-man, frat-house vibes, but this place is so…grown up."

I let out a laugh, knowing the exact kind of bachelor pads he's talking about.

I gather my belongings, and we head out to my car to begin our twenty-five-minute ride.

"This is your mom's boyfriend's house, right?"

"Yes. Byron is kind of stuffy, but so is my mother. I guess they're a good match. They've been together for a few months."

"I've gathered you don't get along with her?"

"I do, but I'm closer to my grandmother. The two of them are like oil and water though. I'm usually the referee. They grew up very comfortable. While my grandmother always remained humble, my mother didn't."

"And your father?"

"He remarried. Three times. He lives in London now. I usually visit once a year if I can. What about your family? Besides your sister in Connecticut."

"I'm originally from Arizona. Both of my parents are still in that area. They both date but no one too serious for either of them. I just have the one sister in Connecticut, no other siblings."

"What brought you to the East Coast?"

He shifts uncomfortably. "Work."

"Work? Can't you do your job anywhere?"

"I suppose I visited and liked the area. And my sister is nearby."

"Does that mean you're not a true Philly football fan?" I smile. "I might have to fire you as a client."

He points to his sweatshirt, which is a Philly football sweatshirt. "I've been converted."

"Phew. You can stay."

He chuckles. "Today I'm going to work on my burgeoning book-boyfriend skills. I appreciate all the advice, and now I need to take it out for a test drive. You're good with that, right?"

"Yes. I was thinking about it. It will be helpful for you to practice, and my mother is always on my case about getting married. It's easier for her to think we're dating. It's a win-win."

"Does she try to set you up? My mother used to do that all the time."

"I won't even entertain that notion. I shiver to think of the type of men she'd choose. She thinks I sit home at night on my computer writing love stories instead of living one. This will get her off my back for a little while."

He tips his hat. "Glad to be of service, ma'am."

I wiggle my eyebrows. "The fake dating trope is a big one. I've written a few books on it."

He chuckles. "Gotcha."

Thirty minutes later, we pull up to the address Mom gave me. It's as ostentatious as I assumed it would be. It looks like Versailles in Paris. This guy thinks he's French royalty. Knowing my mother, he very well might be.

As we walk to the front door, Trey takes my hand in his. It's huge. I could fit five of my hands in his. I look down in question though I don't pull away.

"Practice, right? You said book boyfriends are all about the constant contact and subtle touches."

"Right. Got it. Thanks again for coming. It's really nice of you to give up your day off."

He smiles. "There's nothing else I'd rather be doing." He sounds so genuine when he says that.

We're introduced to a handful of people, including Byron's daughter, Amelie. She's an attractive blonde, a few years younger than me. She eye-fucks the shit out of Trey. I suppose I don't blame her.

We also meet her boyfriend. He's a good-looking guy, but he has nothing on Trey.

Byron's friend, Andrew, stares at Trey for a long time. "Do I know you? You look very familiar."

Trey shakes his head and turns his face away just a bit. "Not that I am aware of."

I lean over to Trey and quietly ask, "Do you see how Amelie is staring at you like she wants to devour you?"

He turns to look at her, and she licks her lips suggestively. *Very* suggestively.

"I didn't until you mentioned it."

I lift my eyebrow. "Already a good book boyfriend. No woman wants a man looking at other women while they're on a date."

"That seems like an obvious one."

Mom fawns all over Trey. She whispers in my ear, "He's so handsome. My grandchildren will be gorgeous."

I roll my eyes. For crying out loud, she's already got us having kids.

"Does he work in finance like Aiden?"

"Mom, he's—"

Before I can finish, Byron pulls Mom's hand. "Let's head out to the pool area. Lunch will be served soon."

We make our way to the indoor pool room. It's more than a room. I let out a laugh when we enter what can best be described as a giant atrium. It's an indoor space that's made to look like it's outdoors. It's practically a courtyard in a glass enclosure. There are larger and smaller tables. There must be at least twenty chaise lounges. The pool has rock formations, a diving board, a slide, and a waterfall.

Trey looks around wide-eyed. "Wow, this is nuts."

We drop our bags on a chair and Trey removes his shirt. What in the ever-loving fuck? He's ripped. His muscles have muscles. He has one of those V-lines into his swim trunks. I don't think I've ever seen that on a real man, only cover model men.

He's so hot. I have to turn around so I'm not obviously drooling over him.

I'm about to unzip my velvet sweatshirt when I feel his heat behind me. "Let me do that for you, baby." He whispers in my ear, "I'm practicing, remember?"

I nod before he slowly unzips my top in a manner that can best be described as erotic. His hands brush across my stomach, and he kisses my neck while doing it. My whole body shivers from his unexpected contact.

He bends and removes my matching bottoms. His fingers run down my legs as he does so. It suddenly feels extremely hot in here.

I look down. My nipples might poke a hole in the bathing suit. I did opt for a one-piece. It seemed silly to wear a bikini indoors. It's white with ruffles. It's very pretty but does little to hide how turned on I am by his touch.

With his hands on my waist, he turns me around and moves his eyes up and down my body. He breathes, "You're so beautiful."

I swallow. "Umm…you don't have to say that. No one can hear you."

He looks down at me as his eyes meet mine. "Would you prefer I shout it?"

Before I can answer, Amelie walks over to us in the smallest bikini I've ever seen. Her nipples are bigger than the tiny triangles attempting to cover them. She holds out her bottle of suntan lotion. "Trey, would you mind putting this on my back? I can't reach."

She turns her back in encouragement. Oh my god. She's wearing a freakin' thong. Is that really necessary for an indoor pool party?

Trey doesn't break eye contact with me as he replies, "We're indoors. You don't need any."

She scrunches her face. "Oh...well...it's moisturizer too. I tend to get dry in the colder months."

Again, not breaking eye contact with me, he says, "Then ask your boyfriend. I'm busy." He turns his head to her and gives her an icy stare. "I don't make it a habit of touching women who aren't my girlfriend. I'm also not a fan of childish, obvious games. I'm here with Gemma today. Respect that and be on your way."

Her face falls in horror and she practically stomps away.

I think I'm panting. Is this Trey or him trying to be a book boyfriend? Either way, I don't think he needs my services. He's got being a sexy book boyfriend down cold. He could write the fucking manual.

Byron and Mom approach us. Mom looks me up and down. "Pretty suit, Gemma. It looks nice on you. Where did you get it?"

I snap out of my Trey trance and turn to her. "Thanks, Mom. I bought it in the South of France last year."

Trey stands next to me and wraps his arm around my shoulder as he pulls me close. "She looks good in everything, doesn't she? I've never met a woman who always looks so perfect. She could make a garbage bag fashionable and sexy."

Mom raises an eyebrow. "Let's hope we never have to find out."

Byron smiles. "What is it you do, Trey?"

"I own a plumbing business."

Mom's face immediately falls. "Oh. Not your normal type, Gemma."

I'm suddenly feeling defensive of Trey and annoyed with my

mother. I wrap my arm around Trey's waist. Fucking hell, his body is rock solid.

"The usual type hasn't worked out so well for me. I'm changing things up."

She gives a disapproving nod. I know exactly what she's thinking. Ugh.

Amelie's scream breaks my heated stare down with my mother.

"Ahh." She whines, "Daddy, the pool is freezing."

Byron turns his head toward her. "What? The heater should keep it warm."

She's got her feet on the first step. "It's ice cold. I think I have frostbite."

He walks over and sticks his hand in. "What the dickens? There's no heat coming out of the jets. Of course the pool guy isn't here today." He looks at Trey. "You're a plumber. Maybe you can take a look at the equipment."

Trey's jaw tightens. I shake my head. "Byron, he's a plumber, not a pool man. I don't think it's the same."

Byron waves his hand. "Nonsense. It's all pipes with water and the like. Right, Trey?"

"Umm…well…I don't have my tools."

Byron smiles. "We have a maintenance shed. Anything you could possibly want should be in there. Come. I'll show you."

TREY

Oh. Fuck. I know nothing about plumbing and even less about pools.

Gemma squeezes my arm. "You don't have to do this."

I don't want to let her down or blow my cover. Smiling, I respond, "I'll do the best I can. I've never worked on a pool, but it can't hurt to have a look at things."

Maybe I'll get lucky.

She nods. "I'll come with you."

"No, no. You all stay here." I kiss her head, taking in her delicious floral-scented shampoo. "Have a drink, and I'll be back as soon as I can."

Byron gathers me a bunch of tools. I doubt I could tell you the name of a single one of them. I don't have a handy bone in my body. The maintenance man in my building has to come and change my light bulbs.

He offers to assist me in the pool equipment room, but I tell him it's better for me to do it alone. I make up some excuse about it being dangerous, like it's a minefield and not a pool equipment room.

As I walk toward the equipment area, I quickly pull out my phone and click on Cheetah's phone number. He answers right away, "I want to wear you like a pair of sunglasses. One leg over each ear."

"What the fuck, dude?"

He fumbles with the phone. "Oh shit. I thought it was one of my dial-a-fucks, Trina. I don't have my contact lenses in. What's up, Trey?"

"I'm at the pool party I mentioned. The pool heater broke, and they think I can fix it because I'm supposed to be a plumber. I don't know what to do. I know jack shit about plumbing and pool equipment."

He starts laughing hysterically. "Oh my god. This is priceless. Why are you calling me? I'm not a fucking pool boy, though I played one once for a chick I was seeing who liked when I dressed up."

"What did you wear? What's a pool boy uniform?"

"A neon-pink banana hammock. Duh."

"I don't know why I ask. Do you know any plumbers or pool people? Please. I need help."

"Hmm. My cousin down in Mexico has a pool. Want me to ask him?"

"Yes, I'm desperate."

"Hold on. I'll conference him in."

I arrive at the pool equipment area with the tool kit in tow. I hear the phone ringing, indicating that Cheetah is calling his cousin.

A man answers, saying something in Spanish.

Cheetah happily responds, "Coma estas, Miguel?"

They start conversing in Spanish. I don't know what the hell they're saying.

"Trey, Miguel said to make sure the heater power is on and then feel the top of it to see if it's hot."

"What the fuck does a pool heater look like?"

After another Spanish exchange, he says, "It will be the biggest rectangular box in the pool equipment area. Like a washing machine. Pipes should be coming out of it and leading to the pool."

I look around and locate what must be the heater. "Okay. I see it." I check the panel. "The power is on." I feel the top, but it's not hot. "It's not hot though."

They start talking again, leaving me clueless.

"He thinks it's probably a pilot light issue. He said to check the gas line."

"I'm not fucking with the gas line. I don't want to cause an explosion. Dying isn't on my list of activities for today."

"Hmm. Fair point."

They chat back and forth.

"Miguel wants to know if you have a wrench."

I look through the toolbox and locate several. "Yes. I have lots. What size?"

"He said to get a big one."

I find the biggest one and pull it out of the box. "Okay. Now what?"

"He said to hit the top of the heater with it."

"Are you fucking with me?"

"No. He said that works sometimes when all else fails. It needs a little kick in the ass for the pilot light to ignite."

"This is stupid."

"What other choice do you have? Just do it."

I tap the top of the heater.

I hear Cheetah sigh. "You're a fucking ball player. Hit the damn heater like you mean it."

I rear back and slam the top of the heater with the wrench three times...and it fucking kicks on. I can hear the pilot flicker on and then see the gaseous heat radiating from the large machine.

"Holy shit. That worked. Cheetah, you're a genius."

He chuckles. "I can't believe that worked. I mostly just wanted to see if you'd do it. Gracias, Miguel."

I concur, "Gracias, Miguel."

"De nada."

I'm feeling about a thousand feet tall right now. That's the handiest thing I've ever done in my life.

With my chest puffed out, I head back around to the pool with a big smile on my face. I look at Byron. "All fixed."

He holds out his hand for me to shake. "Good man. How about a little whiskey to thank you. I have a special collection you might like."

"I'm fine hanging with Gemma. Thank you though."

Her back is to me as she talks with a group of people. I approach and place my hand on her lower back. I notice goosebumps erupt over her skin.

I lean into her. "We're back in business."

She looks surprised. "You were able to fix it?"

I smile. "Yep."

Just then a man walks over to me with a silver tray full of the smallest ice cream cones I've ever seen. I'm talking one-inch-sized ice cream cones with some sort of sorbet on them.

In French-accented English, the man asks, "Amuse-bouche, sir?"

I look at Gemma and pinch my eyebrows together. "Did he say *amused bush?*"

She lets out a loud laugh. "No, amuse-bouche. It's kind of a small, bite-sized appetizer. But sorbet is more of an intermezzo even though we haven't eaten yet."

"What's an intermezzo?"

She bites back a smile. "It's like a palette cleanser you have between meals."

I blow out a breath. "I need to up my fancy-talk game."

I grab two and feed her one before popping the other in my mouth. It's pretty good.

I nod in contentment. "My bush is amused."

She giggles.

I learned a few more new fancy terms today. Like side dishes are called accompaniments.

What I really learned is that I love having my hands on Gemma's body. I may have gone overboard in taking advantage of this opportunity, but I couldn't help myself.

GEMMA

I get home, immediately send Trey on his way, and run straight into the bathroom to turn on my shower. I need it to be ice cold. My body couldn't be any hotter if it were on fire, and it has nothing to do with the high temperature of the indoor pool area.

Trey's hands were on my body all fucking day. All. Fucking. Day. I swear, he maintained constant contact every single second. He held my hand, touched my back, squeezed my hips, and ran his fingertips up and down my arms. Even when we had lunch, his arm was around my chair while he gently tickled my shoulder. And when he wiped the salad dressing from the corner of my mouth with his thumb, I swear, I almost had an orgasm.

I've never in my life been given more singular attention from a man than by my fake boyfriend for the day.

He managed to charm every single person there. Even my mother liked him by the end of the afternoon. This guy absolutely doesn't need my services, but right now, I need to be serviced.

I undress and grab one of my preferred waterproof toys, setting it on the shower bench. After stepping into the shower, I begin to wash my body with the fragrant shower gel. I scrub ferociously, needing to erase his touch from my memory before I implode from it. Closing my eyes, I can still feel him. It's like he's imprinted on me.

His blue eyes were drinking me in all day. That chin dimple was taunting me. I'm not sure what I want to do more, lick it, or sit on it.

I run my hands over my thighs. The palm of my hand brushes between my legs. I jerk at the sensation. Why am I suddenly wondering what Trey's calloused hands would feel like between my legs? Oh god, I bet they would feel amazing.

My fingers run through my wet folds while I imagine what it would have felt like if Trey slipped his fingers into my bathing suit. Admittedly, I found myself praying for it most of the afternoon.

I lift one of my feet onto the bench, spreading my legs wider. Looking at the tile wall, I get flashes of Trey fucking me against it. He's got the size and strength to easily fuck a woman against a wall. That's another book-boyfriend thing that's hard to replicate in real life, but I have no doubt Trey could accomplish it.

My fingers now slip inside myself. They're too soft. Too small. What if they were more like his fingers? God, I want to know what that feels like. I'm aching for it.

Better yet, what if his cock was inside me? There's no way a man his size isn't well-hung. He must be at least six feet, three inches, and every single part of him is thick. I can't help but imagine his girthy cock sliding in and out of me.

I think of his blue eyes and the intensity with which they stared at me all day. He made me feel like the most cherished person in the world.

And his body. I bite my lip hard. His body is a dream. I want to run my fingers over that V. I want to trace the hair from his belly button that disappeared into his bathing suit.

I slide my now vibrating toy inside me while my fingers travel to my clit. It's swollen, as it has been most of the day. I move the toy in and out with one hand while the other rubs until I feel the orgasm building.

Squeezing my eyes shut, Trey's face is on my mind when I fall over the edge. It goes on and on, seemingly unending. I haven't had this powerful of an orgasm in a long time.

Shit. I need to stay away from him. It's Thanksgiving next week. He'll be easy to avoid. After that, I'm going to tell him that he doesn't need my services. It's for the best.

CHAPTER
Seven

GEMMA HAS MOSTLY IGNORED me for over two weeks. I thought the first week was because of Thanksgiving, but it's been more than a week since that, and aside from a few short telephone conversations and texts, she's barely communicated with me. She's definitely pushing me away.

Maybe I came on too strong at the pool party. Or worse, maybe she's met someone else.

After a good amount of nudging, she agreed to meet me for a drink after work today. I'm getting dressed when Layton knocks at my door. I shout, "Come in."

"Hey, man. Cheetah and I are heading to Club Liberty tonight. We're trying to talk Tanner into coming. He's been wallowing in misery at his new house. Want to come?"

"Sorry, I can't. I have a date with Gemma."

"A date?"

I scrunch my nose. "A meeting. If, by chance, it ends early, I'll text you and come by."

He nods. "How's it going with her?"

I sigh. "I thought it was going well, but she's practically ghosted me for two weeks."

He shrugs. "It's the holiday season. Everyone has shit going on. For what it's worth, I think it's cool that you're so into her and you're doing something about it."

"You do? You guys are always busting my balls about it."

"Nah. We're just jealous that you found a good one. It's not easy. I hope it works out." He wiggles his eyebrows. "How's your dick?"

"Finally all healed. I've tested the pipes a few times. He's ready for duty when called upon."

He chuckles. "I hope you get to take it out for a real test run soon."

I let out a laugh. "Me too."

WHEN I ARRIVE at the bar, I see her in a circular booth with her vodka martini and a beer that I hope is for me. Some guy is standing at the table talking to her. Stay cool, Trey. Don't bash his face in.

As I get closer, I can hear her trying to blow him off. She's not into him.

She notices me and gives me a huge smile. That's a good sign. But then she says, "There's my boyfriend. I told you he was coming. It was nice to meet you. Have a good night." She looks at me. "Hi, honey." She holds up the beer. "I ordered you your favorite beer."

I happily play my part. "Hey, baby." I lean over and softly kiss her cheek. "I missed you today."

Why does she always smell so good?

The guy finally walks away, and she breathes a sigh of relief. "Thanks for that. He wouldn't take no for an answer."

"My pleasure."

I slide into the booth, wanting to sit right next to her, but knowing that I should probably leave a little bit of space between us for now.

I get a look at her body. She's in a short skirt, a sweater, and knee-high boots. So sexy.

I blow out a breath. "Glad to finally see you. I thought you were ignoring me."

She gives me a clearly fake smile. "Sorry. It's been a crazy couple of weeks. I've been busy with work, writing, and holiday shopping lately."

I let out a nervous laugh. "Good. I thought you were firing me as a client."

She bites her lip nervously. "That's the thing, Trey." She swallows. "I don't think you need me. You're a good guy. You're an attentive boyfriend. Even as my fake boyfriend you handled everything perfectly. I don't want to take your money anymore. Jenna would be crazy not to fall for you just as you are."

She looks pained as she says it. I don't know what to make of it.

I'm about to protest when I see her eyes widen and her lips turn down. "Oh, shit."

"What's wrong?"

She mumbles, "My ex just walked in with a woman."

I subtly turn and see a typical Wall Street-looking asshat in a fancy suit walking through the door with a smug smile.

I look back at her. "Are you still hung up on him?"

She immediately shakes her head. "No. Not even a little bit. I know our parting was for the best. It's just hurtful that he moved on so quickly. He's been parading a bevy of women around town, in all the places he knows I hang out, since the day we broke up. Meanwhile I've been alone for the entirety of the six months. It stings a little. That's all."

I hate seeing her hurt like this. I say the first thing that comes to mind. "Use me."

She pinches her eyebrows together. "What?"

"Use me. Pretend we're together. I'll be your fake boyfriend. Again."

I see her internally debating while he makes his way over toward us with a cheap copy of Gemma on his arm. Without any further hesitation, I do what I've been dying to do since the second I first laid eyes on her. I slide toward her, grab her face, and smash my lips to hers. It's much more aggressive than I would normally offer for a first kiss, but I've been waiting to do this for a long time, and I simply can't help myself.

She lets out a slight yelp in surprise before quickly giving in. *More* than giving in. She fists my shirt and pulls me toward her.

Her face and full lips are so damn soft. I'm afraid my scruff will hurt her, but my fears are quickly set aside the second she moans into my mouth.

I slide my tongue past her luscious lips, tasting as much of them as I can on my way. Her tongue meets mine before she slips it into my mouth.

Her lips are like the sweetest candy I've ever had. They're moving against mine as pure lust overcomes my body. I want to tear her clothes off and touch her everywhere. Maintaining control is no small feat.

One thing is perfectly clear to me. If I wasn't before, I'm officially a goner for this woman. The way she kisses me back will now ruin me for all other kisses.

My cock is straining against my zipper. The piercing is rubbing in both a good and bad way. I would burn this place down just for the possibility of being inside her right now.

She rotates her hips toward me, sliding her bare leg across my lap. Her knee gently brushes over my cock. Oh fuuuuuck.

My hand runs up the back of her leg, under her skirt, until it reaches her ass. It's smooth and bare. She's wearing a thong. She's so fucking sexy.

I hear someone calling her name. It feels faint and from a

distance, but it's not. It's right at our damn table. Go away, dickhead. I'm in the middle of the most epic first kiss that ever was.

Screw him. I grab her neck with my other hand and deepen the kiss. Her hands pull me as close to her as possible. She's as absorbed in the kiss as I am.

He calls her name again and our kiss breaks, but our lips remain close to each other's. Hers are big and kiss swollen. Her red lipstick is smeared around her lips and she's panting. It may be the hottest image I've ever seen.

Even with her name being called, we don't break eye contact. She simply breathes, "Trey." It's so soft that only I can hear it. She felt everything I did with that kiss. I know it. I'm not alone in this.

"Gemma, are you there? Hellooooo?"

That breaks both of us out of our trances. We turn our heads to see the ex-boyfriend standing there with a nasty snarl on his face. I can't believe Gemma dated this guy. He's not nearly good enough for her.

She slides her leg off me until she's seated upright in our booth again. She starts to move away, but I throw my arm around her and keep her close. Our legs are touching. She looks down at where they meet and bites her lower lip.

She then takes a breath before looking up at him and forcing out a smile. "Aiden, what a surprise. How are you?"

His eyes toggle between us before they land on me. "You look familiar."

Shit.

He holds out his hand. "I'm Aiden. And you are?"

I shake his hand back. Hard. "Gemma's boyfriend. I've never heard your name before. Do you two work together?"

Aiden seems taken aback that I haven't heard of him. I inwardly laugh as I run my fingers down Gemma's arm. She shivers and her eyes flutter.

Gemma shakes her head. "Aiden and I used to date. It was a long time ago."

She reaches over with her thumb to wipe her lipstick from my face, which I have no doubt is everywhere given the current condition of her lips.

I grab her wrist to stop her and gently kiss the inside of it. "Don't wipe it off, baby. I wear your lipstick proudly."

I make a show of licking all around my lips. "Hmm. Tastes so good. Just like the rest of you."

Her eyes are hooded with lust as she stares up at me with a flushed face. I bet this is what she looks like when she comes. I ache to see the real thing.

We're definitely having a moment. At least we are until the shithead clears his throat again. "Gemma, can I talk with you for a moment? Privately."

Before she can answer, I shake my head. "Nope. When you have a girl like Gemma, you never let her out of your sight. Do you have any idea how many guys want her? Look at her. She's fucking perfect. I like to keep her close. Anything you have to say to her you can say in front of me."

He judgmentally looks down at my jeans and T-shirt. "What is it you do, Mr...."

"Donatucci. You can call me...Mr. Donatucci. I'm a small business owner."

"What type of small business?"

"The business of making Gemma happy."

I give him a big, exaggerated smile. Gemma lets out a small giggle.

His face twitches before he returns his attention to Gemma. "I'm serious. Can we talk?"

Gemma sighs. "What about? There's nothing for us to talk about. Honestly, anything you have to say can be said in front of my boyfriend. We're on a date, and you're being rude."

I give her a squeeze. I'm proud of her for that.

He slowly nods before looking at me again. "Do you know what it is that she does for a living?"

"Of course. She's a talented lawyer."

"Are you aware of her...side project?"

"That she's an equally talented romance author? Hell yes, I am." I point to myself. "Luckiest guy ever. I love it when she puts me to work on intimate scenes she's writing. Being her muse is such a high. And her books are amazing."

He has an unimpressed look on his face.

She looks at me with shock written all over her beautiful face. "You've read them?"

I gently rub her face. "Of course, baby. I've read every single word you've written. You're brilliant." I turn back to Aiden. "I hit the lottery with this one. Any man would be crazy to ever let her go. I know I never will."

I lean over and kiss her neck in three spots. Goosebumps spread all over her skin as she practically melts into me.

I can't help but inhale deeply. "Fuck, baby, you smell so good. I've got a new scene in mind for tonight. I can't wait to get you to myself."

She lets out something between a whimper and a sigh. Looking up at me through her long lashes, she breathes, "You do?"

I nod. "I've been dreaming it up for a *long* time."

She's entirely focused on me, forgetting that Aiden is standing at the table. She runs her thumb over my chin dimple before leaning in and kissing it. She then kisses her way up until her lips meet mine again. Softly at first, but when her fingers thread through my hair, she deepens it.

Uncaring where we are, she throws one leg over me, rubbing her body on mine. I run my hands under her skirt and grab her hips, pulling her until she completely straddles me.

And then it's game on. She unashamedly rubs her body on mine. I squeeze her ass and push her onto me. I can feel the heat of her pussy on my rock-solid cock, which is begging to be inside her.

Her nails deliciously scrape across my scalp. This is fucking hot.

She mumbles into my mouth, "Touch me, Trey." She circles her hips. "I want you to touch me."

I open an eye to make sure Aiden is gone, which he is, and then I immediately move my hand along her inner thigh until I find her center. Her panties are soaked. "Are you wet for me?"

She nods. "Yes. Please. I *need* you to touch me. I'm aching for you." She mumbles, "I've *been* aching for you."

With my hand hidden under her skirt, I slide her panties to the side and run my finger through her before slowly slipping it into her. She immediately clenches around me.

"Baby, you're so wet and so tight." I push in further. "Is this what you need? You want to come on my fingers?"

She pivots her hips, deepening my finger inside her. She breathes, "Oh god, Trey. Don't stop."

I love that she's taking what she needs from me. It says a lot for the type of lover I know she'll be. I equally love that she doesn't give a shit that we're in the middle of a crowded restaurant.

I add another finger and pump it in and out of her, eventually adding my thumb over her clit. Her pussy is bare and she's moaning loudly into my mouth.

Kissing my way to her ear, I whisper, "Do you have any idea how long I've wanted you? The first time I saw you in those pink silk pajamas. The way your eyes sparkled when you laughed. I've watched that video a thousand times while touching myself. The first time we met in person was when you were in the green suit. It matched your eyes. And then you were wearing that white bathing suit. My cock was hard all day while I touched your beautiful body."

Her body clenches around my fingers so damn tight. She

pulls my hair as she buries her face in my neck and drowns out the sounds of her orgasm.

Her body goes limp over mine and she breathes heavily. We're silent for a few minutes as she comes down off her high.

Her fingers eventually move down to my zipper, but I grab her wrist. "Not here."

She breathes, "Where?"

It's not like I have my own place in Philly, and I can't take her to Layton's three-million-dollar penthouse.

"Let's go to your place. It's close by."

She nods but doesn't otherwise move. "I need another minute. My legs are numb."

I hold her, loving having her in my arms for the first time. Kissing along her neck, I say, "Take as long as you need. I can't wait to make you feel that way again."

We sit there silently for a few minutes while I take liberties with my hands. They roam up her bare back and all over her long legs. And my lips never leave her body.

At some point, her head pops up and her adorable, perfectly manicured eyebrows furrow. "Oh my god. What about Jenna?"

I tuck her hair behind her ear. "I'm sorry, but there is no Jenna. I made her up to spend time with you. It's always been about you."

GEMMA

"There is no Jenna. I made her up to spend time with you. It's always been about you."

His handsome face is a mixture of lust and uncertainty. If I had any use of my legs, I'd walk out. But they're numb from the intense orgasm he just gave me.

I have mixed emotions over this. What he did in front of

Aiden was special. And I certainly can't deny that I'm attracted to him. But he's been lying to me. I can't start up with another liar.

As the feeling comes back to my legs, I try to move away but he holds me in place. I fruitlessly push against his chest. "Trey, let me go."

"I don't want to."

"You lied to me. That's a trigger for me."

He doesn't loosen his hold.

"Trey. Now."

He begrudgingly releases me, and I push away from him. "I need to go."

I reach into my purse for my wallet, but he stops me. "I've got it."

"Fine." I stand while he quickly pulls out his wallet and throws two hundred-dollar bills on the table.

What the fuck? We had two drinks.

I don't have the mental energy for this. I turn and make my way toward the door with him hot on my heels. "Gemma, stop. Let me explain."

"Go away, Trey."

I push through the front doors and out onto the street when he grabs my arm. "No, I will not go away. I'm in love with you."

That stops me dead in my tracks and I turn back to him. "What? What did you just say?"

He runs his fingers through his hair. The same thick, wavy hair I grabbed onto through my explosive orgasm.

"I...I have insta-love."

I scoff. "It's not a medical condition, Trey. It's a fucking made-up romance novel term. It doesn't exist in real life."

"Let me assure you, it does. I saw your drunken video with your friends and my whole fucking life flashed before my eyes. Everything was clear. I want you in my life. I...I love you."

I shout, "Insta-love doesn't exist! Most of the romance tropes don't exist in real life. Hell, half of them are felonies. It's all a damn fantasy. It's not real."

"That one exists."

"So you lied to me? All this time, were you just learning things I like so you could get into my pants? Mission accomplished."

"It's not about getting into your pants. It's about getting into your heart. I applied so I could spend time with you and get to know you. It went from infatuation to full-fledged love. You're perfect. I want you in every single way."

I stand there dumbfounded. Opening and closing my mouth a few times, I'm left speechless.

I have no words for this insanity. The only thing I can think to do is to walk away, so I do.

My brownstone is nearby. I walk as fast as I can in my high heels though he's never far behind.

I walk up the steps toward my front door. When I reach it, I turn around with tears in my eyes. "This whole situation is messed up. Leave me alone."

He puts his face in mine. I can smell his intoxicating Trey breath. The look he gives me is the type I write about, not the type that exists in real life.

He reaches for my face, brushing his thumb over my lips. "Tell me you didn't feel it when we kissed. Tell me you weren't thinking what I was thinking."

I croak out, "What were you thinking?"

He leans down and brushes his lips over mine as he whispers, "That it was my last first kiss."

I gasp. That's exactly what I was thinking. At the time, I felt ridiculous for even considering it.

Before I know what's happening, his mouth is on mine again, and I lose all train of thought. I've never been kissed this way before. Apparently, I've only been kissed by boys my whole life because Trey kisses like a man. Everything about him is manly. His body, his smell, his words, his possessive touch. It's a drug

I've resisted, thinking he wanted someone else, but she doesn't exist. He wants me.

His big hands move all over me like he can't get enough. Like I'm *his* drug.

My body is thrumming with anticipation for what else he can do to me. What he just did to me at the bar was an appetizer of everything that's been playing out in my mind for weeks.

He kisses me so deeply and passionately that it's almost too much to bear. For some reason, I know his words aren't hollow. Whether they're possible or not, I know he means what he said to me.

Grabbing my keys from my hand without breaking the kiss, he unlocks and opens my front door.

It closes behind us after we walk through, and he pushes me up against the door. He kisses down my body until he's on his knees in front of me. Grabbing my hips, he buries his nose in my stomach and inhales deeply.

Eventually, he looks up at me with his blue eyes that convey nothing but sincerity. "I'm not asking for anything but a chance. Give me a chance to win you over. Let me love you."

I run my fingers through his hair, needing to touch him. I can't manage to not touch him.

I feel like I'm at a crossroads. I hate how things began with lies, but I equally can't deny the attraction to him. If nothing else, I'm curious what this intense heat between us can produce in the bedroom.

As he stands to his full height, towering over me, I do the only thing I'm capable of doing right now. I remove my shirt and toss it to the floor. He scrunches his face. "I wanted to rip that off you like in your second book."

I can't help but smile. "You *really* read all my books?"

"Cover to cover. Every single page. Every single word." He thumps his head. "I've committed all your fantasies to memory. I'm going to make every single one of them come true."

"Then you'll remember the scene where *she* did this." I

proceed to rip open his shirt, and I hear the buttons scatter all over the floor. I've always wanted to do that.

He growls in response like the man did in my book.

The corners of my mouth turn up slightly. "Be a good book boyfriend and growl louder for me. I want to feel the vibrations between my legs."

His tongue slips out and runs along his lower lip before he growls loudly and lifts my legs until they're wrapped around him.

He takes both my wrists into one of his big hands and pins them above my head. "Oh, sweetheart, you have no idea the lengths I'll go to just to make your fantasies come true. But you're about to find out."

He roughly pulls down my bra and stares at my breasts. His jaw goes slack, and he briefly closes his eyes. When he opens them, he cups one of my breasts in his big, rough hand. The callouses send tremors down my body. Why are they so fucking hot? I need to add this feature to the men in my books. Writing about men with soft hands is now a thing of the past. Rough hands are my new kink.

"I've spent hours wondering what your nipples look like. In my wildest dreams, they were never this perfect."

He bends his head and teases one with his tongue before wrapping his lips around it and sucking it into his mouth. My eyelids flutter. Fuck, that feels good. It's an electric current straight to my clit, making it pulse with need.

I grind onto him, desperate for the friction. I'm shamelessly rubbing against him like I did in the restaurant. Why am I so ravenous for him?

He lifts his head. "Where's the bedroom?"

I point down the hallway. "Third door."

He locks his lips to mine again as he moves us toward my bedroom. We crash through the door, and he tosses me down onto my bed. He stands over me in all his beautiful glory. I take in his chest and abs. After we were at the pool party, I dreamed about tracing every muscle with my tongue. I can't wait to make it my reality.

He slowly removes the remnants of his shirt before unbuckling, unzipping, and removing his jeans. He stands there in his boxer briefs with an exceedingly large and hard cock threatening to break through.

His eyes meet mine. "Grand romantic gestures, Gemma. I've listened to every word you've said since the moment I met you."

He slips his thumbs into the sides of his boxer briefs and slides them down his legs. I audibly gasp as his cock springs free. I suck in a breath in a way I didn't know was possible because I don't think I've ever been more shocked in my life.

Yes, he has a book-boyfriend-worthy cock, but that's not the object of my shock. I sort of expected that given his size. It's the jewelry on the tip of said cock. He's got a fucking Prince Albert piercing.

"Just like you said you wanted."

"Wh…wh…when did I tell you that?"

"I heard you on the phone with your friend, telling her that you wanted a man with a pierced cock."

I point at it. My voice and hand shake as I ask with uncertainty, "And you had one already, right?"

He smirks as he swivels his head from side to side. "Nope. The first night we met, I went and had this done. It's the first of what promises to be many grand romantic gestures I do for you. Only you."

"You…you put an extra hole in your dick for me?"

He chuckles. "I did."

I'm speechless. For the first time in my life, I'm speechless. My mouth moves up and down, but nothing comes out. I think I'm in shock.

He gives his dick three long pumps. It's so fucking erotic that I don't know what to do with myself. I've never in my life been this turned on. It's like every nerve ending in me is enhanced.

The second he touches any part of my body, there's a good chance I'll come.

I point at it and ask the dumbest question I've ever asked, "Have you had sex with it yet?"

He rolls his eyes. "No, Gemma. I didn't get my dick pierced for you only to use it on someone else. The only woman who will ever feel it is you. I assume you've been with a man who has a piercing before, right?"

"No," I shout. "I haven't! I was messing around with my friend when you eavesdropped. Dick piercings are for book boyfriends. I don't know any real men with them. It's a fantasy, not real life."

His jaw drops and he breathes, "Holy shit."

I cover my mouth. "Oh my god! I don't know what to say. I'm overwhelmed. I can't believe you did this…for me."

He takes a few long breaths. "Forget about the piercing. It's done. This is about us. You and me. Tell me that you can't wait to feel me moving inside your body. That you've wanted it for nearly as long as I have." He places his hand over his heart. "Tell me I'm not alone in feeling this magnetic pull to you."

I flash back to the second I laid eyes on him. He's gorgeous. Of course I was attracted to him, but he was my client. He wanted someone else. At least I thought he did.

"Maybe we should stop. You're my client." I run my fingers through my hair. "I'm so confused."

He smirks. "You're fired. Are you happy now?"

I blow out a long breath. "I feel it, Trey, I do. I'm a little scared right now. You've said and done a lot of things. I feel so much pressure."

"Don't. Put it all out of your mind and give in to the moment." He leans over and kisses the corner of my mouth. And then the other corner. And then my neck. It immediately soothes me.

This would actually be a sweet, tender moment if his giant, hard, *pierced* dick wasn't bobbing between us.

He grabs my face. "Here's what's going to happen. I'm going to finish undressing you so I can properly worship your body. Then I'm going to wrap my lips around your pretty pussy and make you come again. After that, my cock will slide inside you so we can both experience something neither of us have before."

I...I...I have no words, so I mindlessly nod my head in agreement because...well...that sounds like a damn good plan.

He reaches behind me and expertly unclasps my bra. It falls away. He stares at my breasts as he rubs my nipples with his thumbs. They harden under his intense gaze and touch.

His fingers then brush over the sides of my breasts and down past my waist and hips until he removes my boots, followed by my skirt and panties.

His eyes move down my body as he grabs his now leaking cock. "You're so fucking beautiful, Gemma. I've never seen anything so perfect."

I feel the same way looking at his body.

His lips meet mine again while he gradually and gently falls on top of me. I wrap my arms and legs around him as our tongues meet and explore each other's mouths through mutual moans.

His cock lays heavy between my legs, dipping in and out of my wetness. I thrust my hips up and he exhales a loud groan.

His hands leave no inch of my body untouched. His lips, tongue, and teeth explore my mouth like he can't get enough of it.

I spend most evenings alone in the dark writing about women being impossibly turned on by fictitious men. Men who I've created in my mind to be the type I think I'd want. Until this moment, I've never felt half of what they get to feel. Lust runs through every vein in my body. My skin heats, suddenly burning for him. It feels like I'll die if I don't have him inside me soon.

He whispers into my mouth, "Do you feel it?"

I can't deny it. "Yes, I feel it." How could I not?

He licks a path down my neck to my chest. His deliciously textured hands grab my breasts while he alternates licking and sucking each nipple with a reverence I've never dreamed possible.

His lips work their way down my body, making good on his promise to worship every part of me. His hands slowly follow suit until they're between my thighs, spreading them apart, pinning them to the bed. His face hovers over my center. I can feel his hot breath teasing me.

My doubts of moments ago are a distant memory. I'm on fire with the need for his mouth to be on me. I try to wiggle, desperate for contact, but he's too strong. *So fucking strong.*

I'm panting like a dog in heat, desperate for him to touch me. The anticipation has me trembling for him.

He licks his lips. "I've been dreaming of feasting on this pussy every damn night since I first saw you. So pink. So perfect." He slowly licks through me. "So delicious."

The tip of his tongue teases my clit for what feels like hours but is likely only seconds. His full tongue finally finds my clit and applies just the right amount of pressure.

His fingers push into my entrance, starting off slowly and then gradually going faster and deeper.

"Oh god, Trey." I fist the sheets and practically push my pussy into his face. I can feel the sensation of his scruff on my inner thighs. I'm going to come in world-record time.

What I thought earlier about Trey kissing like a man when I've clearly only kissed boys in the past, also goes for the way he eats me. He's a man devouring my body and playing it perfectly.

I usually like to be on top when a man goes down on me so I can control the pace and depth, but I don't need to with him. It's as if he knows everything I need and everything I didn't know I needed.

He continues his heavenly movements. I'm writhing all over the place. "Please don't stop."

His eyes meet mine and convey more than I can bear right

now. We make eye contact as he sucks my clit hard and curls his fingers in just the right spot. I feel like a bomb is going off between my legs. I yell out as my body opens up and erupts like a volcano. This orgasm is even more intense than the one I had in the restaurant.

My vision is spotted, but I feel the sudden coldness of him pulling his face away from my center, then I feel him move up my body and position his tip at my entrance.

I still haven't regained my vision, but I manage to mumble, "Condom."

He grunts, "No," as he rolls his hips and pushes into me. "Nothing between us. Ever. I'm going to fuck you so hard and deep, you'll be feeling me for days. You won't be able to walk."

I can feel my body spasming around him, ignited by his dirty words and never having come down fully from my recent orgasm.

My mind begs me to grab a condom. A man like Trey has undoubtedly been with countless women. But holy fuck, that piercing. It drags through me, hitting every right spot along the way. I lose my breath at the sensation. I know we should stop, but my greedy whore body would rather die than have this feeling end.

I can only manage the super eloquent, "Holy shit. Don't stop. Don't ever stop."

He pushes all the way in, brings his forehead to mine, and breathes, "I'll never stop. You're mine. For good."

Between his words, his size, and that piercing, I feel so damn full of all things Trey.

He momentarily pauses and looks at me. I think he's actually asking permission to proceed. I lose my internal battle of sense and wrap myself around him, wanting to keep him close. Digging my ankles into his ass, I grit out, "Fuck me," as I encourage him to begin his movements.

His lips take mine again. I can taste my orgasm on his tongue. So fucking hot.

He pulls out and then slams back in. Holy hell. This is going to be epic.

As he establishes a rhythm, my eyes roll around in my head at what must be the greatest pleasure in existence. He's a skilled lover and that piercing is blowing my mind.

I swivel my hips and arch my back, trying to give as much as I'm getting. If the sounds he's making are any indication, he's more than enjoying himself.

"You feel so fucking good, baby. Open up for me again. Let me feel your pussy come on my cock, beautiful girl. *My* beautiful girl."

He somehow manages to fuck me and make love to me at the same time. It's hard and wild yet still tender and loving. I don't know how he's achieving that balance, but he is. It's almost too much to bear. How can our first time be this intense? How can we connect on the highest of levels while barely knowing each other?

His tongue and lips are everywhere. His big hands manage to work my body over like he's committing it to memory, always leaving a blazing trail in their wake.

I'm two more orgasms into this when I feel his thrusts become more erratic.

I breathe, "Don't come inside me."

"But—"

"I mean it." I might be in outer space right now, but I have some limits.

His face is buried in my neck. "I want to come inside your body. I need to mark you as mine."

"You can come in my mouth."

That gets his attention. He pulls out of me, shifts up my body, and thrusts his massive cock into my mouth. I lick around the piercing before grabbing his ass and pushing him as far in as I can take him. I can feel the metal against the back of my throat.

"Oh fuck, Gemma. Oh shit. I'm coming."

If I didn't have a giant cock down my throat, I'd tell him to give it all to me. But I do, in fact, have a mammoth pierced cock clogging up my throat.

He grunts loudly as hot creaminess fills my mouth, sliding down with ease. He yells out my name throughout his entire orgasm. I wrap my lips tight and suck every last drop.

After I finish swallowing it down, he collapses next to me, pulling my overheated, sweaty body close to his. Out of breath, he practically moans, "That was amazing. I knew you'd blow my mind."

Me? I barely did anything. He's the one who blew *my* mind.

I can feel our joint heart rates beating erratically against each other. There's something deeply intimate about them falling in perfect sync with one another.

Once I can form a sentence, I ask, "How was your orgasm with the piercing? Umm…you know…for research." I bite my lip. "Use descriptive words."

He smiles as his hands move all over my body. "Best of my life, but that may have been my sexy partner."

"Any other words just in case a certain author wants to describe the male point of view in a book of hers? Adjectives are welcome."

He chuckles. "Like a bomb went off between my legs and I couldn't see straight. I think I blacked out for a few seconds."

Yep, I know the feeling. Also, I'm totally using that in a book.

He pulls me so I'm fully on top of him. He's so strong. Manhandling me is second nature to him. Oh my god, I sound like a romance novel. Trey is an actual book boyfriend come to life. I feel like I'm in the movie *Weird Science* where the guys created the perfect woman on their computer and she suddenly appears. It's like I've written the most perfect man and now it's manifesting itself in Trey. Well, except for the lying. I certainly don't write men who lie.

I rest my chin on his chest and look up at him. "Condoms if you ever want to do that again."

His face falls. "Aren't you on birth control?"

"Yes, I have an IUD, but we're relative strangers, Trey."

"This isn't casual sex for me."

"I know. You've more than made that clear, but I hardly know anything substantive about you. I don't know how many partners you've had. Judging by your performance, I'm guessing it's been more than a few. When was the last time you had sex?"

"I haven't had sex since you posted that video. I promise that I have a clean bill of health."

"Hmm."

I mindlessly trace his chin dimple with my finger, entranced by it. "How many women have sat on this?"

"None that matter." He mock bites that finger. "You like the cleft, don't you?"

"Umm hmm. It's so sexy. It's one of the first things I noticed about you."

He runs his hands over my lower back and ass, giving me chills. "My friends always make fun of it. Since I was a kid."

"They're jealous. I promise you, women love it."

I reach my head up and lick through it. "Yum. I can taste me on it."

I feel him harden under me.

I giggle into his chest. "Only book boyfriends have three-minute turnaround times. There's no way you can go again this quickly."

He wiggles so I can feel just how hard he is. "Why don't you sit on it and find out? I've been trained to be a book boyfriend by the best in the business."

I smile as I lift my body onto his and then place his tip at my entrance. My safe sex talk is already forgotten. I'll make him put a condom on in a minute. I just want to feel this again for a little bit. Nothing has ever felt better.

Slowly sinking down on him, I moan in delight.

He teases my nipples, but his eyes are focused on where our bodies are joined. "What does the piercing feel like for you?" He smirks. "Use descriptive words. You know…for research."

My eyelids flutter. "Like the stairway to heaven. Like I can't believe I went nearly thirty years without it. Like you're ruining me for all other men."

He lifts an eyebrow. "There will be no other men. Ever."

I bring my body up and then slide back down on him. "One day at a time, Romeo. One day at a time."

CHAPTER
Eight

TREY

I WAKE in the morning to Gemma in my arms. I never want to wake up without her again, but I've come on very strong. Toning it down a drop might be a good idea. I don't want to completely freak her out…more than I already have.

I pull her close and pepper kisses all over her bare back. She coos, "Hmm. I could get used to this."

I run my hand down her body and over her hips and legs, enjoying her sexy curves. "Me too. You have a gorgeous body. I'm obsessed with it."

My mind flashes to the way she felt when we went at it several times throughout the night. I'm insatiable for her. The only thing standing in our way now is the truth about who I am. I need to figure out a way to tell her, but she went into a whole thing last night about being lied to. I'm nervous, though I suppose it's now or never.

I'm about to break down the final barrier between us when her cell phone begins ringing. She sleepily reaches over and mindlessly accepts the call. I hear an older woman's voice. "Gemma Morgan, I can't see your pretty face."

Gemma pops up, the sheet falling to her waist, exposing her gorgeous tits. "Shit."

I ask, "Who's that?"

She covers my mouth with her hand but it's too late.

The voice on the phone asks, "Gemma, is that a man I hear? Let me see his face. Let me see both your faces."

Gemma falls back and lets out a breath. After pulling the blanket up to make sure our naked bodies are covered, she turns the phone until a much older woman comes into view. "Good morning, Grammy Jane. This is Trey. Trey, this is Grammy Jane, my grandmother."

She smiles at me, and I do the same to her. "Gemma has your beautiful eyes, Grammy Jane. Can I call you that?"

"You can call me anything you want, sugar lips. Are you responsible for that big smile on Gemma's face?"

I can't help but grin. "I sure hope so."

"I'm guessing that you're the plumber, right?"

I wince. Ugh. More people who believe the lie. "I'm the lucky man your granddaughter is spending time with."

Grammy Jane rubs her hands together in excitement. "I'm so glad you finally unclogged her pipes. Trust me, she needed it. And she's been crushing on you for weeks."

Through gritted teeth, Gemma scolds, "Grammy Jane, not now."

I chuckle. "I've been crushing on her since the second I laid eyes on her, but tell me more about her crush."

Gemma interrupts, "I'll have you committed to a nursing home if you say one more word, old lady."

Her grandmother laughs before picking up her glasses, placing them on her face, and looking more closely at the phone. "You look familiar, Trey. Have we met before?"

Now, with her grandmother on the phone, isn't the time for the big reveal. I try to divert the conversation. "I'd remember a beautiful woman like you, Grammy Jane."

She giggles in glee. Gemma leans over and kisses my shoulder while rubbing my back appreciatively.

I squirm as I start to harden at her touch. Gemma notices through the blanket and attempts to discreetly hide it from the camera.

Grammy Jane, who seemingly misses nothing, says, "Oh, pft. There's nothing I haven't seen before. If he doesn't have to fix his matrimonial peacemaker when you touch him, the chemistry isn't there."

Gemma lets out a loud laugh. "Matrimonial peacemaker? Classic. I'm using that in a book. Grammy Jane, why don't I call you later today?"

"I understand. If I had that hunk in my bed, I wouldn't be on the phone either."

I wave at the camera. "It was nice to meet you, Grammy Jane. Next time I'll wear a shirt," I mumble, "and pants."

"I'd prefer you didn't."

Gemma rolls her eyes. "Goodbye, crazy old lady."

"I need to talk to you. Be sure to call back." She gives Gemma a knowing look as something passes between them.

She ends the call and sinks her head into my chest. "Ugh. That was embarrassing. She's going to be relentless with the questions when I call her back."

"You two are obviously close."

"She's my best friend. I know that's weird because she's my grandmother, but she's been there for me in ways no one else ever has."

I lift her chin. "I think it's sweet. I can't wait to meet her. She lives in Florida, right?"

"Yes. I'm going down there for a week over Christmas. Her friends are a hoot. I get a kick out of all of them. They give me a ton of material for my books."

"What? Old people give you book material?"

She smiles. "Older communities are a secret hotbed of

sexual behavior. Did you know that they have higher than average STD rates in those communities?"

"Are you serious?"

"Yep. And they all know what I write because my grandmother brags about it. They want their salacious stories in my books. I swear, half of them go out of their way to have crazy sex just so they can report it to me. Being down there is a riot."

"That's amazing. I'm coming with you this year. I want to meet your grandmother and her friends."

She sighs toward the ceiling as she pulls away from me. "Trey, let's take a step back. I'm not even sure what we are."

"I think I've made my intentions clear, Gemma. I'm almost thirty. I'm not interested in immature games or nonsense. I want to be with you."

"No games, Trey? What do you call signing up for my book-boyfriend service just to get into my pants? Don't bullshit me. You've been playing a game this whole time. At least have the dignity to own it."

She's not wrong. In my mind I've been focused on her, but I can't deny the truth in her words.

She tosses the blanket toward me and gets out of bed. "I need to shower and get to work. I'm already late."

I grab her arm. "Gemma—"

She pulls away. "I like you. I really do, but my boyfriend when I was in law school was a bullshitter. He was the *I see a future with you* guy while he was sleeping with someone else. I agree, we're both too old for games. I'm not the one playing them. Our entire relationship has been a fake one. You've been faking *everything*. It's some weird variation on the fake dating trope I use in my books."

"I'm not faking my feelings. Everything I said to you yesterday was honest. I want to be with you. Whatever it takes."

"Actions speak louder than words. I want to build things the right way, slowly, based on trust and honesty, not invite you to my grandmother's house for Christmas before we've even gone on a real date."

Now definitely isn't the best time to tell her I'm not a plumber and I don't even live in Philadelphia.

"Fine. When can I take you out on a date?"

"I've got a busy week at work. I'm sure you're busy too. How about this weekend? Saturday night?"

My shoulders fall. "That's, like, four days from now. Why not Friday?"

"I have plans with my friends Val and CJ on Friday."

I sigh.

She lifts her eyebrows. "Yes or no for Saturday?"

I furrow my brow. "You're standing there naked. I can't focus."

She grabs my shirt from the floor and slings it around her body.

"Now you're standing in my shirt. It's so hot."

She blows out a breath and crosses her arms. She's so damn cute when she pouts.

With a protruding lip that matches hers, I mumble, "Fine. Four days."

I'M IN THE COUGARS' batting cages practicing with Cheetah and Layton. Cheetah is sitting with me while Layton is swinging at pitches. "How's it going with Tami Maida?"

Layton stops and wiggles his eyebrows up and down. "He didn't come home last night. I'm guessing it's going *very* well."

I shake my head. "I'm not talking about that stuff with you guys. She's going to be my wife and the mother of my children. Off-limits."

Cheetah makes a puking noise. "Ahh. Tone it down, dude. You're treading into dangerous over-possessive stalker-trope territory. Tami won't like you if you act all crazy. Isn't she supposed to be training you to be a good book boyfriend? This isn't book-boyfriend behavior. This is psycho behavior, though I suppose some women get off on that too."

"I know who I want and I'm going after her. It's hard to put into words what it feels like. I know in my gut that she's the one for me. And her name is Gemma, not Tami. It's going well. She knows I was a fake client and that I'm interested in her."

"Does she know you're a fake plumber?"

I lean my head back in despair. "No. I was going to tell her this morning, but we got interrupted. She's very hung up on the fact that I lied to her about being a client. I wimped out on telling her the rest. I'm not sure she can handle it yet."

He slaps his forehead. "This is such a classic romance novel story barreling headfirst toward a third-act breakup because you didn't tell her the truth of your identity."

"What the fuck is a third-act breakup?"

"Romance novels are split into three acts. The first act has them meeting or re-meeting. There's attraction plus a bunch of drama and a general foundation to the story. Sometimes there's a misunderstanding or some other obstacle in their way. It's usually exciting and builds up anticipation. The second act has a ton of sex. Whatever has been building between the lead characters explodes. Things are good. Authors drop hints that some other shit might go down, but us romance readers are optimistic. We pray it's all a red herring and that nothing bad happens. Unfortunately, it *always* does. You can't be happy for two straight acts. That goes against romance novel formulas. Then we get to the third act. Some big fucking dramatic event happens. In most books, they break up because of it. Not all, but most. Sometimes they face obstacles together. I enjoy that change of pace from time to time. But usually, they break up."

I run my fingers through my hair, feeling panicked. "Fuck. I don't want to break up. They always get back together, right?"

He shrugs. "Most of the time. Sometimes it's heartbreaking

and painful. I've read a few that don't have happily ever afters. I'm in bed for days, crying my eyes out when I read those."

"What's an example of something that causes a third-act breakup?"

He deadpans. "Lying. Miscommunication. Anything deceitful. Does any of this ring a bell? I'm sorry to be the one to tell you, but you're definitely headed for a third-act breakup."

My shoulders fall. "Shit. How do I avoid it?"

He twists his lips. "Well, the worst thing is for her to find out the truth from someone else, not you. That makes it harder. You *have* to be the one to tell her. It's your best shot at no third-act breakup."

Layton walks out of the cage. "Maybe she won't be upset. Dating a baseball player is a turn-on for a lot of women." He smirks. "I would know."

He and Cheetah high-five, but then I get a whiff of a nasty smell. "Lancaster, your batting glove stinks."

Cheetah chuckles. "If his hand smells from sweating, how do you think his dick feels right about now in this hot as fuck room?"

I smile. These guys are too funny sometimes.

I don't know what to do to avoid our third-act breakup. I'm thinking maybe I need her to fall madly in love with me so she'll never want to break up. If she's in love and then I gently slip in that I'm a professional baseball player worth millions of dollars, perhaps it won't be as bad as Cheetah thinks. After all, those are romance novels. They necessitate drama. This is real life. We don't need a dramatic event.

Incidentally, I'm also thinking that I need all the second-act sex I can get.

GEMMA

It's late morning and I'm fruitlessly working on a contract. I can't get my evening with Trey out of my mind. The highlights keep replaying like a movie trailer. The hottest sex of my life. Where do I go from here?

The way he touched me. The way he worshiped me. The way he made me come…over and over again.

I fan my face. Is it getting hot in here?

I slowly run my fingers over my desk. Darian and Jackson always have sex in her office. I've never even considered it for myself. I almost laugh at the notion of Aiden and I having sex on my desk. He'd be all uptight about the papers and files.

Two years with Aiden, and I never wanted him half as much as I wanted Trey. *Still* want Trey.

How did I let myself go twenty-nine years without the type of passion I shared with him in one single night? As a romance author, I'm disappointed in myself.

I begin imagining what a romance book scene would be like in my office with Trey. I would kill to have him take me right here. To bend me over all my files and fuck me senseless while the papers fly all over the place and neither of us gives a shit. I make a mental note to write an office sex scene tonight while the fantasy is fresh in my mind.

I'm running through all the small details of what it would look like when my cell phone buzzes. I pick it up to see that it's our *Perverts* group.

Libby: What's the best lube on the market? JoJo and Ava need not answer. I know Gemma probably has them ranked somewhere.

JoJo: Not me with a bowl of popcorn waiting for the answer from Gemma.

Ava: Yep. This is going to be epic. Gemma, you were born to answer this question.

Me: Well, if you must know… I prefer überlube. It works well and is easier to wash off afterward than other, more popular lubes like Astroglide. It also doesn't stain your sheets. Beginners often like Intimate Earth Ease because it also relaxes the anal opening, but I don't care for it.

Libby: Because your anus is plenty relaxed.

Me: Don't knock fifth base 'til you try it, Lubey Libby. If you don't like actual oil, you can use SUTIL. It's water-based, but it doesn't work as well.

Libby: überlube for the win.

Me: And it's on Amazon. You can have it in hours in case of emergency…so I've heard.

JoJo: Emergency anal. That's a new one.

Me: When you want it, you want it.

Our silly texts are interrupted by Andrew buzzing me from the front desk. "Ms. Fairchild, there's someone here to see you."

In a brief moment of panic, I glance at my calendar, fearing I have a meeting that I forgot about. As I thought, I don't have any appointments scheduled. I press the intercom button. "Who is it?"

"He said to tell you it's the piercing police."

I can't help the smile that forms and the thrill that shoots through me. "I'll be right there."

After taking a quick glance at myself in my compact mirror, I open my office door and practically sprint toward the reception area. Trey comes into view wearing nice black slacks and a blue button-down shirt. The sleeves are rolled up. His forearms are so damn muscular. I suppose it's not surprising given what he does for a living, but they're just so big and sexy. He's simply…yummy.

My mind flashes to what the rest of his body looks like under those clothes. Complete and total perfection.

As I approach, Andrew discreetly hangs his tongue out and pants like a dog. He mouths to me, "Holy fuck."

I ignore him and look at the sex god standing in my office. "Trey? What are you doing here?"

He lifts what appears to be a takeout bag. "Since you got a late start today, I thought you might be skipping lunch. I brought you food."

"That was thoughtful." I motion for him to follow me. "Let's eat in my office."

Not caring that my coworkers can see us, he immediately takes my hand in his and kisses my cheek before saying, "You look gorgeous."

I take in my royal-blue cascaded wrap dress. "Thank you. You look nice too. You don't wear those clothes to work, do you?"

"I…umm…just had some busy work in the office today."

The second we walk through my office door, he drops the food on the ground, closes the door, and pins me against it. I let out a small yelp in surprise before his lips meet mine for a deep kiss.

I feel every hard ridge of his body pressed against me. His hands ride up the backs of my thighs, and then he lifts me and pulls my legs around him. My dress is naturally lifted to my waist. His hardness is pushing against my center, igniting me immediately.

He nibbles and bites down my neck. "You smell so good. I can't stop thinking about you. About us."

I grab onto his thick hair and grind myself against his erection. I breathe, "What happened to four days and a real date?"

"I'll give you whatever you want. Just one more time to hold me over. I can't get enough of you." He pulls my thong to the side from behind me and slips a finger inside me. "You're soaking wet for me."

"You make me this way."

"I need to be back inside you."

My pussy contracts around his finger. I'm sore from last night yet aching for more of the best sex of my life.

I let out a small moan. "I've been thinking about you all morning." I glance over to my desk, wanting the full fantasy that's been running through my mind. "Bend me over and fuck me across my desk."

I both hear and feel a deep rumble in his chest as he pulls away from the door and moves us toward my desk. He's already tearing a condom wrapper open with his teeth.

I look up at him. "Don't be gentle."

After setting me down, he roughly turns me around and shoves my front over my desk, just as I imagined it. He pushes my dress further up my waist and rips my thong away before slamming his giant cock inside me.

Yes, just what I wanted.

It feels amazing but not as good as it did without the condom. Wanting the scene I imagined to be epic, I turn my head back. "Take it off. Fuck me bare again."

Yes, my brain isn't functioning. Have I mentioned that the sexiest man alive, who happens to have an enormous, pierced cock, is inside my body right now?

Within seconds, he's withdrawn, I see the condom flying across the room, and then he slams back into me.

I let out a loud moan. "Fuck, yes. So good."

He grabs my hips with bruising strength and begins his long, deep, hard thrusts. "You like me bare inside you, baby?"

"Y-yes." I don't know if his cock was sent from heaven or hell, but either way, I'm going along for this ride.

That fucking piercing has got my mind spinning. I can't see straight. I'm so incredibly turned on.

"Your pussy is greedy. She's squeezing me." He slaps my ass. "Such a good pussy."

I grab onto the far edge of my desk so I have some leverage to push back onto him.

The sounds of my wetness and his body slapping hard against mine are loud. My desk slides an inch or two with every hard thrust.

He's giving my body a pounding that I never want to stop.

He leans over, first biting and then sucking hard on my shoulder. I let out a scream.

"That's right. Show everyone in this office what I'm doing to you. Who you belong to."

What real-life man talks like that? And, damn, I'm loving it.

My climax is already churning through me. My toes are numb. This is romance book hot. I can't believe it's my reality.

His fingers dig hard into my hips again. I look back at his body. Somehow his muscles ripple through his shirt. I didn't know that was possible. His jaw is tense, completely absorbed in this. I love how into the moment he is.

He notices my turned head and grabs me by the hair. Hard. His skillful tongue plunders into my mouth while his cock ravages my body in a way I've never known before.

I tear my eyes away to see files and papers flying everywhere. Holy shit. I think I manifested this whole scene.

I've got one more aspect of the scene I had in mind that needs to happen. I breathe, "My ass. Put your fingers in my ass."

He lets out a loud groan before I hear him suck on his fingers, then he circles my back entrance and slips them in.

"Fuck, yes. I like it deep."

He pushes his fingers all the way in while continuing to ram into me hard with his cock.

My orgasm builds and builds until I can't possibly hold it back. As if sensing it, he leans over and seals his mouth over mine. I yell into him as the freight train of an orgasm crashes and then ripples through my entire body, completely shattering me.

"You want me to fill you with my come? Mark you as mine?"

"Yes!"

He growls, "Oh fuck," as he pushes in deep and fills me with his warm seed.

Collapsing on top of me, he gently kisses my shoulder. We're both breathing heavily. He pants, "I like your office. It's nice."

I giggle. "What color is my carpeting?"

I feel him smile on my shoulder. "I have no idea. You're completely bare."

I let out a laugh. "Not *that* carpeting."

He pulls everything out and turns me around. I see his handsome, smiling face.

He runs his thumb over my sensitive lips. "You're all I see, Gemma."

Leaning forward, he sucks my lower lip into his mouth. My nipples harden. I'm about to deepen the kiss when I feel his come trickling down the inside of my thigh.

I pull away and look down. He notices my line of sight and runs his finger through our joint fluids before holding it up to my mouth. I wrap my lips around his finger and suck it clean, all without breaking eye contact.

His jaw slackens and he immediately hardens again. I can't deny that I get off on the effect I have on him.

I reach down to touch him, but he grabs my wrist. "Later. Let me take care of you."

He pulls up his pants and walks into my private bathroom, returning a few moments later with a dampened hand towel. Propping me on the desk and spreading my legs, he runs the warm towel through me until I'm thoroughly cleaned, with a tenderness that's more dangerous for me than anything he's said or done.

I can't help but run my fingertips through his stubble. "I fantasized about this very scene."

He nods as he pulls my dress back down over my legs. "I know. It was in your fourth book."

"No, that scene was fade to black. I mean minutes before you arrived, I was thinking about it. I wanted *you* to throw me over my desk and have your wicked way with me. I've never done it, and I was sitting here imagining it when the receptionist buzzed me."

He pinches his eyebrows together. "You haven't had office sex before?"

I shake my head. "I haven't done most of the things I've written about."

"It's time to change that. You said there are hundreds of tropes. Give me some that might interest you in reality."

I smile at this fun little game. "Let me think. The professor-student trope is hot as hell." I channel my inner sex goddess and breathe, "I want to be a naughty student."

His pupils dilate and he adjusts himself. He's so sexual.

He croaks out, "What else?"

I bite my lip. "I wouldn't mind a little primal play."

"What's that?"

"It can be kind of broad because it generally means letting go of societal norms, but I mean it more predatory. I want to be hunted. Stalked. Like I said, half the tropes are felonies. It doesn't mean they can't be hot as hell."

His cock is fully straining against his black pants. He takes a few deep breaths before retrieving the bag of food. "I have to feed you. You'll need your energy for the things I have planned for you this weekend."

I can't help but smile as we lay out the food in my sitting area and sit down to enjoy the meal.

I open the boxes and find it's tacos. My face lights up. "Tacos? You know the way to a woman's heart."

He mock flips his hair and in a girly voice, says, "It's Tuesday. You *have* to eat tacos on Tuesdays. It's practically the law."

I giggle at him referencing a direct line from one of my books. He really did read them. Does it get more perfect than Trey?

"I can't deny the truth of that statement. Taco Tuesdays should be a national holiday."

He smiles.

"Tell me more about your sister."

His smile widens. It's obvious that they're close.

"Her name is Diana. She and her wife, Sherrece, own a restaurant. Diana went to culinary school and she's an amazing chef, but she's taken a step back since having kids. Sherrece manages the restaurant. She's originally from New Zealand."

"Does she speak Kiwi?"

"She does. Her accent is still heavy even though she's been here for fifteen years."

"When she says the word *six*, does it sound like *sex*?"

He chuckles. "It does. How do you know that?"

"I dated a rugby player from New Zealand years ago. It always made me giggle. Tell me more about them."

"Their kids are Maggie and Leo. They're amazing. I go up when I can but FaceTime with them a lot. Since you're ditching me until Saturday, I might head up for a night or two tomorrow."

"I'm not ditching you. I said we'd get together over the weekend. That's reasonable."

"Hmm."

"Will you spend Christmas with them?"

He nods. "Yes. I think my mother is coming in too. I know you're going down to Florida. Does anyone else in your family go too?"

"My mother was supposed to come, but she and Byron are heading overseas for the holiday. It's all for the best. She and my grandmother have a love-hate relationship."

"Are you more like your mom or grandmother?"

"I suppose I have my mother's sense of style, but I hope I'm more like my grandmother in every other way. She has this love of life. This try-anything-and-everything attitude. I wouldn't be writing if not for her. My mother is embarrassed by it. She thinks writing romance novels is beneath me. My grandmother loves that I put myself out there like that. She sees how happy it makes me."

"You should always do what makes you happy."

"I try. I let you fuck me without a condom again. I was happy in that moment even though I should be committed for doing it."

He lets out a laugh. "I love how brash you are. And sex with you makes me *extremely* happy."

"What else makes you happy?"

"The fact that I met you."

"Such a charmer. You're too perfect. Tell me something imperfect about you."

He twists his lips. "Hmm. I'll tell you something, but you have to promise not to tell anyone. Ever."

I rub my hands together. "Ooh. A big secret. This just got good. Not a word. I promise."

"Trey isn't my real name. My real first name is," he whispers, "DeMontré. My sister calls me Demon Trey."

I burst out laughing. "Are you serious?"

"Sadly, yes. It's French, and my mother was obsessed with European royalty."

"She'd get along with my mother. She thinks she's *actual* European royalty."

"That's why my sister is Diana. She got a normal royal name, and I got a snooty, ridiculous name."

"Oh my god, you're the least snooty person I've ever met. No one snooty fucks like you."

He smiles. "I'll take that as a compliment."

"It was intended as one, Demon Trey."

"I'm going to spank you every time you call me that."

"Spanking is one of my favorite tropes, Demon Trey."

He narrows his eyes at me. "I'm not kidding."

I giggle as I look at him and mouth, "Demon Trey."

He grabs my body and pulls me over his lap.

Spank.

I giggle and shout, "Demon Trey."

Spank.

And that's what leads to another round of office sex, this time with him sitting in my chair.

CHAPTER
Nine

I SIT BACK in the restaurant booth and rub my tummy in complete and total satisfaction. "This is your best stew yet, Lady Di."

My sister smiles warmly. Besides our eyes, we don't look alike at all. She's got much lighter hair and skin tones than me. I resemble my mother, and she resembles my father.

"Thank you. I've been working on a new recipe for our revamped menu."

I look around the mostly busy restaurant. "How's business?"

"Pretty good." She tilts her head and looks at me lovingly. "It's a lot easier when you have no debt."

I bought this building and all the equipment for her so she could open the restaurant without big bills hanging over her head. She worked her ass off for years, sweating as a chef and moving from restaurant to restaurant until she and Sherrece decided to take the plunge and open their own. Their previous lifestyle wasn't conducive to family life, and they were struggling. I'm more than happy to have been able to help create this opportunity for them.

I wink at her. "Isn't that what little brothers are for?"

I rub my nose with Leo's. "Right, buddy? Always take care of the special women in your life."

Diana raises an eyebrow. "Speaking of special ladies, anything new for you in that department?" She has a hopeful look on her face.

I can't help the smile that finds mine.

Her chin drops. "You've met someone?"

"I met *the* one. I have zero doubts. Di, she's incredible. She's smart, funny, sexy, and just…everything."

"Wow, Trey. I've never heard you talk like this."

"I never had a reason to until now."

"Tell me about her."

"She's an attorney and an author. Very smart and upscale. She's easily the most beautiful woman I've ever seen in my life. I love how she's incredibly feminine yet super into sports, but I think my favorite thing about her is that she considers her grandmother her best friend. They have the sweetest relationship."

"Does she work in The City?"

"She works in *a* city."

"What city is that?"

I scrunch my face. "That's the only problem. She lives in Philly and doesn't know I live in New York City."

"Don't people assume that you live in New York considering you play for the Bombers?"

I turn my face, unable to make eye contact. "She doesn't know who I am."

"Trey—"

"Listen, Di, it's hard to be me sometimes."

"An attractive baseball player who's treated like royalty, makes stupid money, and can have any woman he wants? It sounds like a real struggle."

I blow out a breath. "I meant finding women who are interested in Trey the regular guy, not Trey DePaul, the famous baseball player. You know how some of the women can be."

"That's because you look for women in clubs. Not real places."

"Well, I didn't find her in a club. She thinks I'm a plumber and she doesn't care."

"She didn't recognize your name?"

I mumble, "She doesn't know my real last name."

She gives me a flat look of disapproval. "Oh, Trey, this isn't you. You're not a deceitful guy. If she's the one, you need to tell her. She's going to find out eventually."

Sherrece plops down at the table, leans over, and softly kisses Diana's lips. In her accent, she says, "Sorry, love. It's a madhouse in the kitchen tonight. Franco never showed. I just tried your new stew though. It's amazing." She smiles. "Maggie is in the back helping them with desserts." She pops a piece of bread in her mouth. "Catch me up."

Sherrece and my sister have been together since college. She's very tall, nearly my height, and used to have long, dark hair, but now it's blonde and shorter. My sister is curvier while Sherrece is rail thin.

Diana sighs. "The good news is that Trey is in love. The bad news is that he's been lying to her."

Sherrece's eyebrows furrow. "Lying? That's not like you, Trey."

I go on to tell them the whole crazy story. By the time I'm done, they're both speechless.

Sherrece blows out a breath. "You *have* to tell her who you are."

I run my fingers through my hair. "I know. It's just that...I want her to fall in love with me first, so she has no choice but to accept it."

Diana shakes her head. "You're a fucking idiot."

Leo mimics, "Fuck, fuck, fuck."

Diana closes her eyes. "Shit."

Leo then mimics, "Shit, shit, shit."

I can't help but let out a laugh. "Leo, say *go Bombers*."

He looks at me for a moment before saying, "Go Toogars."

Sherrece laughs. For some unknown reason, she's a huge Cougars fan. "I've trained our son well. He'll never be a Bombers fan."

Diana sighs. "You know the right thing to do."

I nod, acknowledging that she's right. "I just need a little more time."

Diana and Sherrece share a disapproving glance with each other.

GEMMA

I fall over on the couch. "Ugh, I can't eat any more pizza."

Val rolls his big brown eyes. "Why are you in nice pants, weirdo? We're watching a basketball game while eating pizza and drinking beer. That calls for old cotton sweatpants."

I scrunch my nose. "I don't think I own any old cotton sweatpants."

CJ lets out a laugh as his shaggy blond hair falls over his handsome face. "How are we still friends?"

I sigh. "I wonder that myself all the time." I look around at the piles of beer cans, dishes, and dirty clothes. "You two live in absolute filth. I can't believe I spend time in this frat house. You both make real money. Get a housekeeper."

CJ lifts one of his ass cheeks and lets out a huge fart. "Ah, much better. I think I'm getting old. Cheese is starting to upset my system."

I shake my head. "You're gross."

"You queefed in front of us last Sunday."

I wave my hand in a dismissive fashion. "Can't prove a thing."

He winks and blows me a kiss. "You love us."

"Hmm. I suppose. It's only because girls are high maintenance. You two are easy."

Val chuckles. "CJ is definitely easy. You should have seen the brown-bagger he was with last weekend."

I shake my head. "Ugh. You know I hate that term. It's so wrong." It's what they've always termed women with attractive bodies and unattractive faces. You put a brown bag over her face, and all is good.

CJ winks at me in his casual hoodie and sweatpants. "They can't all be tens in both face and body like you."

I bat my eyelashes. "You flatter me."

He chugs the rest of his beer, burps loudly, and then asks, "What about your love life? Have you been knocking boots with anyone lately?"

I narrow my eyes at him. "Knocking boots? You're so unoriginal. Even my grandmother and her friends are more creative than that. Come up with something better, and then I'll answer you."

"Doing the dirty deed?"

I toggle my head back and forth in contemplation. "Hmm, better, but not good enough."

Val shouts, "Stuffin' the muffin!"

I smile and nod. "Yes, using food is always good."

CJ thinks for a moment. "Makin' the bacon?"

"Now you two are thinking like writers. So proud of my boys."

They both smile with pride.

I straighten my shoulders. "I am, in fact, riding the Bony Express. Thanks for asking."

CJ laughs. "Bony Express. Good one. It's not another finance dickwad, is it? Our friendship barely survived Aiden."

"Definitely not like Aiden. In fact, he put Aiden in his place earlier this week when we ran into him."

Val wiggles his eyebrows. "I like him already. When are we going to meet him? Ya know, give him the brotherly shakedown."

I smile with affection for my two best friends. I'm fully a guy's girl. I always have been. I simply get along better with men. CJ and Val have been my best friends since middle school. The number of threesome jokes I've endured throughout the years has got to be in the tens of thousands. I don't know why people can't comprehend opposite-sex friendships, especially a tight trio. Never for a single second have any of the three of us entertained the notion of something physical. They see me as one of the guys or even as a sister. It's not that they're unattractive, just the opposite, but it's simply not what we are.

At this point, we mostly watch games together. Sunday football is our weekly tradition, but we'll occasionally do a Friday night basketball game over pizza and beer, like tonight. And on rare occasions, I'll go out to clubs with them. They always go home with random women, so I don't love doing that with them, but watching sports with my two boys is my happy place. It's how I relax.

My phone pings, and I look down at an unfamiliar number. It's photos of me from today. One at work and one while I was on my way to lunch.

I write back.

> Me: Who is this?

> Unknown: A secret admirer.

Huh? A secret admirer? Wait a minute. I smile. I bet it's Trey. I click on Trey's contact information and call him. He answers right away, "Hey, beautiful. I was just thinking about you."

"What were you thinking?"

"Dirtier thoughts than I can admit in my present company."

"Oh, where are you?"

"Still in Connecticut. I'll head out when the kids go to bed. I need my fill of them."

That's sweet. "Oh, I...umm...got a text from an unknown number. I thought it might be you?"

"Nope. Not me. We just finished dinner, and the kids are about to get baths. What are you doing?"

"Watching the basketball game with Val and CJ."

He chuckles. "I love your sporty side. I'm looking forward to tomorrow. Actually, I'm looking forward to Sunday morning."

"Why Sunday morning?"

"Waking up with you in my arms. It's suddenly very lonely when you're not there."

I bite back my smile. "Swoony fucker. Cheez, what did you do, go to some romance book-boyfriend academy?"

He lets out a laugh. "I may have done that, but it doesn't make it any less true. I loved waking up with your naked body pressed to mine. I'm counting the seconds until it happens again."

"It's kind of presumptuous for you to assume that I'll be sleeping with you on our first official date," I joke. "I'm not that kind of girl."

I can hear him step away from the sounds of water running until he's in the quiet.

"Baby, I'm going to be inside your body for so long tomorrow night that you'll be feeling me all week. First, my tongue will taste your sweetness, and then my cock will pound you and fill you with my come. Fuck, I love when I first enter you and your eyes roll back in pleasure. And when you're about to orgasm, your eyes turn a brighter shade of green. You'll be coming over and over again as your juices coat my cock and drip down all over me."

I swallow hard as the thought of all that seems mighty appealing. I look up to see Val and CJ staring at me. I'm undoubtedly red in my very guilty-looking face and smiling like a schoolgirl.

"Answer something for me."

I whisper, "What?"

"Which one makes you more wet, the thought of coming on my tongue or the thought of coming on my cock?"

I shift in my seat and then breathlessly respond, "Both."

I can hear his breathing pick up. "Good, 'cause you're getting both tomorrow night. Speaking of which, I had something sent for you to wear."

"You're picking out my clothes? I'm very particular in that department."

"I know my girl. Just wait until you see it."

I hear a little girl's voice say, "Uncle Twey, huwwy up."

"I'm being summoned to the bath. Tell your girlfriends hello and that I can't wait to meet them. I want to know all things Gemma Fairchild."

Before I can correct him, he hangs up.

I lean my head back on the sofa pillow. Damn, that was hot.

Val and CJ are still staring. I lift my head and take a breath. "Boys, I highly suggest you up your dirty talk game." I fan between my legs with my hand. "Nothing gets a girl wetter than some quality dirty talk."

CJ stands up and throws his arms in the air like he's performing in a play. In a deep voice, he bellows, "Fair maiden, I want to caress your ample bosom."

I shake my head and giggle. "You're a fuckwit. It's not the eighteen hundreds. That's not dirty. I feel bad for the women you date."

Val asks, "What did he say?"

"That he wants to fuck me until I can't walk and then fill me with his come. That he wants my juices leaking all over him. That he can't wait for me to come on both his tongue and cock."

His eyes pop open. "Holy shit. That's some grade-A dirty talk. Maybe I do need to up my game."

I nod. "His dirty talk is off-the-charts hot. And the sex is even better."

CJ asks, "Better than that football player you dated our senior year? What was his name?"

Val answers, "Troy, the quarterback. And he drove a cheesy yellow Trans Am. Tell me you're an eighties high school date rapist without telling me you're an eighties high school date rapist."

I burst into laughter. "Oh my god, that's so funny. And so true. Trans Ams are the official bat signal of pushy guys."

Val smirks and he nods in agreement while CJ raises his eyebrows. "Well? Answer the question."

"Yes, it's way better than Troy. His name is actually Trey. I didn't even think about the similarity. Trey has a magical dick that also happens to be pierced. He blew my mind."

Val looks impressed. "Magical dick, huh? You're not easy to please, so good for Trey."

I pout. "I'm not hard to please."

Val scoffs, "Yes, Princess Gemma, you are. And it's only gotten worse since you started writing because now you create these fake, over-sensationalized men. No real man can ever live up to your fictitious men. That's why you haven't dated a single person in six months."

I contemplate that. Is it true? Am I expecting too much from real-life men due to the perfect men I create?

CJ interrupts my thoughts. "When are we meeting him?"

I scrunch my face. "Not yet. It's new. We have some…obstacles to overcome."

"Like what?"

"Nothing I want to discuss. Let's watch the second half."

They both eye me skeptically. It's rare that I keep anything from them, but I want to talk about this with my grandmother when I see her. She's my voice of reason.

CHAPTER

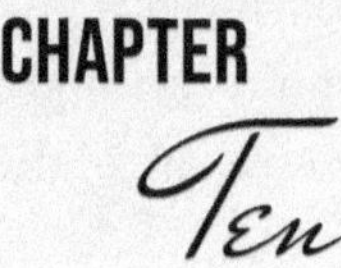

GEMMA

WHEN I GET HOME after the game, there's a big box waiting for me by my front door. I carry it inside and open the intricately wrapped gift. After sifting through all the tissue paper, I find what appears to be a school uniform, but it's actually a designer plaid skirt and blouse with amazing thigh-high leather boots to match.

The accompanying note reads,

A smile finds my lips. He's trying to play into the professor-student trope fantasy I mentioned. He's so cute.

I look at the labels. They're all high-end. He must have dropped a ton of money on this outfit. I hate that he did so, but I can't deny how incredibly sweet and thoughtful he is.

I decide to text him.

> Me: Thanks for the beautiful outfit, Professor Trey. It's a bit much for this shy student.

> Trey: I've been hard since I picked it out, just thinking of how you'll look in it.

> Me: How hard? Remember, I like adjectives.

Even better, he sends a picture with the evidence of his arousal. Fuck, he has a great dick. I save it to my phone. I'll be using this picture in my spank bank for a long while.

> Me: You have a book-boyfriend-worthy dick.

> Trey: You have a book-girlfriend-worthy pussy. So pink and tight. Is it wet right now?

> Me: You'll have to wait to find out, but let's just say that Professor Trey has a PhD in dirty talk.

> Trey: Professor Trey's PhD currently stands for Pretty Hard Dick.

> Me: LOL. I can see that in the photo.

> Trey: When you fuck your vibrator tonight, think of me.

> Me: I intend to. Wishing you were here. Can't wait for the real thing.

> Trey: Just about to leave Connecticut. Now I have to drive for nearly four hours with a boner.

> Me: I'll take care of it tomorrow night. With my tongue.

> Trey: Ugh. You're killing me. Until tomorrow, my love.

I don't respond. His love talk makes me uncomfortable. I much prefer dick pics and dirty talk.

The next day, I wake up to a text from that unknown number again. It's a picture of me carrying the box through my front door last night. I get the chills. What's happening? Who is this? Should I go to the police?

I hide under my blankets for another hour until I decide it's time to be productive. I stay in most of the day writing, suddenly feeling inspired to write a few sex scenes with a dirty-talking pierced man.

In the late afternoon, I shower and head out to do a little shopping before Trey arrives to pick me up. I have a very specific Christmas gift in mind for him. We've obviously just started dating, so I'm not going overboard, but I think he'll get a kick out of it.

I'm walking back to my house when all the hairs on my neck stand at attention. I feel like someone is following me. Quickly turning back, I see no one. Maybe I'm just spooked by the texts from the unknown number. If I receive any more, I'm definitely going to the police.

I hurry home as fast as I can to get ready for our date.

An hour later, there's a knock at my front door. I open it and see Trey wearing khaki pants, a button-down shirt, a bowtie, and a sweater vest. He's looking every bit the part of a professor. Except for the fact that his muscles are so big they look like they're about to burst through the shirt. I didn't have any professors who filled out their clothes quite like this. Hell, I didn't have any who were anywhere near as hot as him.

He's holding a single red rose. My insides liquefy. He remembered what I said about my teenage first date. My best first date. I have a feeling tonight will beat that one.

His eyes shade over with lust as they move up and down my body. The plaid skirt is *very* short. Even with thigh-high boots, there's plenty of skin between my boots and the bottom of the skirt. The blouse leaves little to the imagination. My hair is down and wavy. I decided against the pigtails. We're going for college-age romance, not felony-age romance.

I feign shock. "Professor Trey, what are you doing at my house? What if someone from the school sees you here?"

TREY

In a sexy voice, she breathes, "Professor Trey, what are you doing at my house? What if someone from the school sees you here?"

If I didn't know before, I know now. There is officially no sexier woman in existence than Gemma Fairchild. That outfit is worth the two thousand dollars I dropped on it. I'll buy a new one every day for the rest of my life if this is the outcome.

I charge at her like a bull until she's pinned to the wall. She places her hand on my chest. "Just a kiss, Professor Trey. I don't want you getting fired over me."

I softly run the rose down her forehead, over her nose, across her lips, and then down her neck.

I can see her pulse beating rapidly in her neck. With my other hand, I cup her cheek and then bring my lips to hers. It's been a long few days, and I'm ravenous for my sexpot.

I try to deepen the kiss, but she turns her head and whispers, "Later. It will be more fun if we wait." She rubs her hand over my cock. "The payoff will be worth it." She bats her long eyelashes. "I'll be a good girl, I promise. You can put it anywhere you want tonight, professor."

I suck in a breath. I'm so damn hard. My cock is leaking. I might come in my pants.

She continues, "Here's a little something to tide you over." At that, she hands me a pair of lace panties. "Be a good boy, and I'll let you keep them. I wore them all day."

After bringing them to my nose for a deep inhale, I growl. I don't know where it came from. It's not like I intended to do it, but there's something primal that takes over my body in her presence. I would burn down the world for her.

Her eyes flutter. "You growl like such a good book boyfriend. I might record it for my social media...and my own personal bedside collection."

"What is your bedside collection comprised of?"

"So far, it's just your dick pic from yesterday. I can't wait to add your growl to it though."

I smile before she reaches up to wipe her lipstick from my face. Now it's my turn to pull my head away. "No. Don't wipe it off. I like being marked by you."

I know the lipstick wiping was a big deal for her in her previous relationship. I want her to know how proud I am to have her on my arm...and my face.

"You want red lipstick on your face all night? What will people think?"

I shrug. "Don't care about anyone but you."

Her smile softens. "You're very romantic, Professor Trey."

I grab her hand and run it over my cock. "I have very unromantic things on my mind right now."

"All good things come to those who wait."

"Are you really not wearing panties? The skirt is short."

She gives me a sexy smile. "I guess you'll have to wait and find out."

My fingers are twitching to find out.

She notices and grabs my hand. "Let's go, professor, before I have to slap you with a ruler." She bites her lip. "Better yet, you slap me with that ruler."

This woman.

I made a reservation at a nice restaurant near her place. I don't want her to have any thoughts of coming to my home. It's not like I have one here.

We walk the short distance there. Her face lights up when we arrive. "I love this place." She sighs. "Between the outfit and this restaurant, it's a lot for you to spend on me. You don't need to feel like you have to do that. I'm just as happy with pizza, beer, and a ballgame."

I mock gasp. "It's our first date. I can't have you telling our children that I treated you like anything other than my queen."

She gives me a disapproving look. "No talk of the future or insta-love-affliction disease tonight. Let's be normal, ordinary people, not romance-book-created, unrealistic trope people."

"Baby, I assure you we're very real. But I'm dressed as a professor, and you're dressed as my student. We'll never be ordinary because we're extraordinary."

She smiles softly and leans into my body before standing on her tippy toes to plant a sweet kiss on my lips.

The hostess shows us to our table. I think she knows who I am. She keeps eyeballing me. I hope it doesn't come out tonight. I'm not ready for that just yet.

I've decided that as soon as Gemma gets back from her trip to Florida, I'm going to tell her the truth. I don't want her to leave being upset with me. I'll be there to take all the punches she'll inevitably throw and beg her to forgive me. And that gives me two weeks to make her fall in love with me.

We're seated at a small table with two chairs across from each other. As soon as we both sit, I grab hers from under the table and pull it to me.

She lets out a small screech. "Good lord, you have the domineering-book-boyfriend thing down pat."

"I learned from the best."

"I didn't teach you that."

"You said to sit on the same side of the booth. There's no booth, so I pulled your chair over."

"Hmm. Fair point. That hostess looked like she wanted to eat you for breakfast. It's probably best we sit close together so I can fight her off."

She adorably holds up her fists.

I smirk. "Are you getting territorial?"

She wiggles her eyebrows. "Maybe I am."

"I missed you the past few days."

"I missed you too. How was Connecticut?"

"It was great. My niece and nephew are the cutest kids in the world. He mimics everything my sister says, both the good and bad." I chuckle. "He may have dropped a few F-bombs."

She giggles. "Wow. I can't imagine. And you'll go back up there for Christmas, right?"

I nod. "Yes. My sister and her wife close their restaurant after lunch on Christmas Eve. We exchange a few gifts then, and again in the morning. We make a huge Christmas brunch together in their kitchen. It's our tradition. Even though my sister is the professional chef of the family, we all know our way around the kitchen."

She rubs my arm. "You cook?"

I nod.

"Ooh. Another checkmark in being a top-quality book boyfriend."

I smile. "I suppose."

"Will you see your parents?"

"Definitely. My mother is flying in. She mentioned that my father might come too."

"Together?"

"They're not coming together, but we can still celebrate as a family. They share kids and grandkids. As rough as the years leading up to the divorce were, it was for the better. They're friends now."

"Oh, wow. That's so nice. Especially for your sister with the little ones. My parents struggle to be in the same room. They haven't seen each other in years. I split holidays for my last few years of high school. Then my father moved abroad, so I just visit when I can. Frankly, I prefer holidays with my grandmother over either of them."

"Ahh, the one and only Grammy Jane. Did she interrogate you after I left the other morning?"

She has a guilty look on her face. "I haven't spoken with her. I'll fill her in on us when I fly down."

"What will you guys do down there?"

Her whole face lights up. "It's hard to explain. She and her friends are in their final quarter of life. They've achieved this inner peace with a general mantra of *I don't give a fuck*. They'll do and say whatever they want. They don't worry about hitting the gym, getting their work done, paying mortgages, driving carpool, paying for college, and regular life stuff like that. They're having an unapologetically good time because they simply don't know what tomorrow will bring. YOLO may be a millennial term, but it's the baby boomers who truly embody it."

I squeeze her hand. "What a refreshing perspective."

She nods. "It is. I let all real-world stress slip away when I'm there and get a kick out of watching these people live their best lives…and say whatever comes to their minds."

"What do you do on Christmas Day? Any traditions?"

"Not like yours, but since my grandmother moved to her place in Florida, it's been the same. We eat ourselves into a junk food coma on Christmas Eve. Christmas Day is a huge margarita and musical festival at their pool. They dance and drink all day. Like I said, simply living their best life."

"And you stay for a week?"

"I do. If I have New Year's Eve plans, I'll come home on the thirty-first. If not, I'm equally happy to spend it with them, though most of them are usually snoring by the time the ball drops."

I place my hand on her exposed thigh. "I'm going to need to get my fill of you for the next two weeks to tide me over."

She leans over and nuzzles her nose along my cheek. "I like the sound of that."

"Tell me what other tropes interest you."

She smiles. "You're very into the tropes."

"I'm very into you and your pleasure."

She licks her lower lip. I want to suck it into my mouth. So fucking sexy. "Hmm. Maybe a little expeditionism would be fun."

I pinch my eyebrows together. "Having sex in front of other people? Like in your fourth book?"

She shakes her head. "That's exhibitionism. Expeditionism

is slightly different. You don't get off on people watching you have sex. You get off on the threat of possibly being caught doing some sexual act in public. It's not exactly the same."

I think for a moment as I slide my hand up her inner thigh. "So, if I were to slip my finger inside you right now—" I push a finger inside her and she gasps. "This would be expeditionism?"

Her eyes flutter as she discreetly widens her legs and ensures her lap is covered with her napkin. "Y…yes."

"We've done this before, but I'm all for pleasuring you at the dinner table any time you want it."

The waitress stops at our table. "Can I take your orders?"

Gemma attempts to push my arm away, but I don't budge, continuing the in and out movements. Her whole face is flushed.

As if my fingers aren't inside her pussy, I smile at the waitress and calmly say, "Yes, I'll have the chicken parm." I turn my eyes to Gemma. "Baby, do you want me to order for you?"

She bites her lip and nods.

"She'll have the eggplant parm and we'll share them both. And please bring us two more glasses of wine."

"Sure thing."

As soon as she leaves, Gemma breathes, "Trey."

I lean over so my cheek is next to hers. "This is just an appetizer. We'll call it an amuse-bouche. Later, it will be my cock inside you. The piercing dragging along your inner walls until you can't help but come all over me again and again."

"Oh god."

I look at our tablecloth. Unfortunately, it's not very long. "Next time we have dinner together, we'll go somewhere with floor-length tablecloths."

"Why?"

"So you can crawl on your knees under the table and suck my cock like a good girl."

She buries her face in my neck to drown out her moans.

She truly gets off on my mouth. Before I realize what's happening, she sinks her teeth into my neck while her body shakes, and she comes all over my hand.

She fucking bit me hard. Somehow it makes my cock ooze that much more for her.

After a few more deep breaths into my neck, she lifts her head and looks around. She pulls my fingers out of her and pushes them into my mouth. "Suck my come off your fingers, professor."

While I happily oblige, she reaches her hands under the table and pulls down my zipper. She then takes out my straining cock and proceeds to give me the best hand job of my life.

It's noon on Sunday, and Gemma has forced me to leave her house. She said Sunday afternoons are a sacred time for her and her friends to watch football. I love her sporty side, but I wanted to be with her today.

She mentioned she's not ready for me to meet her friends yet. Admittedly, that hurts, but I tried to act like it didn't bother me. I can't introduce her to my friends either. They're the two biggest stars in Philadelphia.

We had the best evening last night. After the heavy petting session, we laughed and flirted throughout dinner. Then we barely made it back to her place before tearing each other's clothes off for more life-altering sex. I've never shared this type of chemistry and passion with a woman.

It's given me that much more to lose. I'm getting increasingly terrified about our third-act breakup.

I walk into Layton's penthouse. He and Cheetah ordered food, and we're planning on watching football games.

I plop down on the couch. Cheetah looks me up and down. "Hey, loverboy. Are you two married with kids yet?"

I sigh. "I wish. She's going to hate me when she finds out who I am. I should have told her right away."

Cheetah nods. "Told ya so. Such an obvious plotline. What a rookie mistake."

I moan out, "Ahh. This isn't a romance novel. It's my real life. I'm in love with this woman. She's...she's...everything."

Layton asks, "How's the sex?"

"I'm not giving details, but it's easily the best of my life. She loves my dirty talk. I need to up my game. Got any good lines?"

Cheetah's face lights up. "Tell her you're like Crest toothpaste. Nine out of ten dentists recommend you in her mouth."

Layton laughs and I roll my eyes. "That's not dirty talk. That's just a cheesy pickup line. You're clueless."

Layton twists his mouth. "How about milk my winky like a cow?"

I sigh. "I don't know why I bother."

Cheetah asks, "What do you call it when a man talks dirty to a woman?"

"What?"

"Sexual harassment. What do you call it when a woman talks dirty to a man?"

I shrug. "I don't know."

"$19.99 per minute."

I burst out laughing. "That's a good one."

Just then, my text tone pings. I see that it's Gemma and excitedly open it.

> Gemma: My legs are missing you between them.

> Me: Don't make me hard while I'm with my friends.

> Gemma: I can't stop thinking about last night. I think I purred at one point.

I chuckle. She did purr.

Gemma: I didn't shower. I wanted you inside me all day.

Fuuuuck.

Me: We hit several tropes last night. Any more you want to try this week?

Gemma: How about why choose?

I look up at Cheetah. "What's the why choose trope?"
He lifts an eyebrow. "When it's one woman and at least three men."

Me: Are you nuts?

Gemma: LOL. Just busting your balls. You're way too possessive to ever share me with another man. And, baby, you're all the man I need.

Me: Damn straight. When can I see you again?

Gemma: I'm around this week. Let's do something seasonal. Maybe ice skating or that new Christmas trolley.

Me: Anything to spend time with you. Tomorrow night?

Gemma: Okay. See you then.

GEMMA

Trey and I have had the best two weeks. We've spent nearly every night together. We went ice skating, we ate good food, we had plenty to drink, and we even went holiday shopping for our families. There's something extra romantic about doing holiday things with him during this time of the year. I don't think there's a single drop of mistletoe left in the city of Philadelphia that Trey hasn't found and kissed me under.

We decided that we'll recreate Christmas and exchange gifts when I get back from Florida. He talked me into returning on New Year's Eve so we can spend that night together.

I'm leaving for the airport in the morning. This is our last night together for the holiday week. We wanted a cozy evening in since we've been out so much lately. We're watching *Christmas Vacation*, the greatest holiday movie ever created. His head is on my lap, and I'm aimlessly running my fingers through his hair.

The ending movie credits scroll, and he doesn't move. I look down and realize that he's sleeping. I can't help but stare. He's so handsome.

I gently trace his chin dimple with my finger. He stirs and mumbles, "I'm sorry I lied. I love you. Don't leave me."

Tears fill my eyes. I'm falling for him, but I know we have an expiration date.

I LAND IN FLORIDA. I need this week with my grandmother to clear my head. She and I have a lot to talk about.

Even though I usually Uber to her house, she's standing at baggage claim, waiting for me with her arms crossed. I know she's mad. I've been putting off this conversation for weeks, sending her calls to voicemail and minimally responding to her texts.

As I get closer, her green eyes, exactly like my own, find mine. "You've been ignoring me, Gemma Morgan."

I blow out a breath. "I know. I'm sorry. I wanted to talk to you about it in person. And I wasn't ready to face reality just yet."

"Yes, we do have a lot to talk about. We can start with you explaining why you're dating a famous baseball player who's pretending to be a plumber."

Eleven

GEMMA

I LOOK AT GRAMMY JANE. Tears well in my eyes and she immediately pulls me into an embrace.

"Oh, sweetie. What in the world is going on?"

I sink into her comfort. "It's so confusing. I don't know why he lied to me. He's come on so strong, claiming he wants forever, but apparently thinks I'm a moron and don't know who he is. I've been waiting for him to tell me the truth since the first moment I met him, but he's been steadfast in the lie. I don't understand it."

When the famous baseball player Trey DePaul first tapped on my shoulder in the restaurant, I nearly fell out of my seat. You see those guys on television, but seeing someone larger than life in person leaves you speechless. And he's gorgeous. More beautiful than any man I've ever known.

He mentioned being my client. It took me a moment, but I realized he was claiming to be *Trey Donatucci*, my alleged Book Boyfriend Builders client. A plumber. Suddenly the profile picture made sense, and I connected the dots. What I didn't understand was why he signed up for the service.

Curiosity got the better of me, and I decided to play along. After all, he did pay our hefty fee. He was entitled to my service. Who am I to judge why he wanted it?

She questions, "You've never said anything to him letting him know that you know who he is?"

I shake my head. "No. It needs to come from him. Honestly, at first, I thought he was just trying to fly under the radar. He wanted to sign up for my service but didn't want anyone to know he needed it. A famous, handsome baseball player? Women undoubtedly flock to him. The night we met, he gave me a speech about wanting a woman who doesn't care about his job. I felt bad for him. I tried to imagine myself in his shoes. Women probably throw themselves at him for all the wrong reasons, so I decided to see where it went. For weeks, I was helping him learn about how book boyfriends behave. Looking back, I realize he asked a lot of questions about my specific wants and needs."

"How did he end up in your bed?"

"The night before you met him on the call, he kissed me and admitted that he signed up for my service because he was enamored with me. He's so intense about his feelings. He showers me with…love and affection. Constantly."

"It's kind of romantic."

"It's incredibly romantic. *He's* incredibly romantic. He openly and unashamedly professes his love to me all the time, but equally lies to my face about who he is. I don't know what to believe, and I don't understand why he hasn't told me the truth of his identity."

"How do you feel about him?"

Tears fall down my cheeks. "I know it's quick, and I'm usually so rational regarding matters of the heart, but I think I'm falling for him. It feels special, but then I keep going back to the lie."

"How's the sex?"

I let out a laugh through my tears. "You have a one-track mind, and the sex is mind-blowingly good." I let out a breath.

"The chemistry we share is like…like what I write about in my books."

She squeezes me close. "We'll figure this out. I'll take care of my girl this week, and we'll make a plan for the sexy Mr. DePaul."

I hold her tight, taking in her familiar, comforting scent, not wanting to let go. "I'm so glad I'm here. I've missed you."

"Me too. For now, we have lunch with Happy, Millie, and Mortimer."

I smile, feeling my spirits lift immediately. "I'm excited to see them. I can't wait to hear about their shenanigans."

We gather my luggage and drive straight to the clubhouse of her community for our lunch date. Happy is nearing eighty, like my grandmother. She's got a stereotypical, gray grandma-helmet hairstyle. Millie is a few years younger with longer, dark hair that I notice has a lot more gray than last year when I visited. It's usually up in a bun, and she's always dressed nicely. Mortimer dotes on her. He's ex-military, with a big belly and hardly any hair at all.

They each embrace me like I'm their own grandchild. Being here with all of them is always soup for my soul.

Happy, never one to mince words, says, "I hear you've got a sexy man. Tell us about him."

I look at my grandmother, and she gives me a subtle shake of her head. She hasn't told them who he is.

I shrug. "He's definitely a sexy man, but we have a few obstacles. We'll see where it goes." I try to keep it light. "It's very new."

"Is he younger?"

"No. We're the same age. Why?"

She smirks. "Your grandmother has been seeing a younger man for a few weeks." She gives Grammy Jane a cheeky wink.

I turn in mock shock at my grandmother. "It appears you've been keeping secrets too."

She seems unaffected. "You haven't called. I would have told you if you did." She pops a grape into her mouth. "Maybe there's still a little gas left in this old tank."

"Are you in a reverse age-gap romance? Will I be writing your story soon?"

She holds her head up high. "Darling, let me give you some life advice from someone who has been around the block a few times." Without an ounce of shame, she declares, "The hole lasts longer than the pole."

I burst out laughing. "Ohmigod, that's the funniest thing I've ever heard." I quickly pull out my phone to type it in my notes. "That's definitely going in a book."

She grins with pride. "I thought it might. I've been working on it for days."

"Will I get to meet this younger stud?"

She wipes the corners of her mouth. "We'll see. He's away for Christmas but will be back toward the end of the week."

I raise my eyebrow at her, indicating that we'll be discussing this further.

I turn to Happy. "What about you? I heard that Samuel was…excited to see you recently."

"Yes, he was. Maybe I'll give that old coot a chance one of these days."

"Are you playing hard to get?"

"At my age, you risk death by waiting too long. My grandson is coming to visit next week. Perhaps I'll call Samuel after he leaves."

"I haven't seen Christian in ages. How is he?" Her grandson is a few years younger than me.

She twists her lips. "He told me he goes both ways. If I hear that someone goes both ways, I figure it's number one *and* number two. I had to call my son to find out what Christian was talking about."

This crew cracks me up.

My grandmother shrugs. "I had to explain to her what

bisexual means and that it's better to be bisexual. Then you've got a chance at everybody."

I slowly nod. "It's a valid point. I can't argue with the math behind that."

They then spend the rest of lunch telling me crazy stories, hoping a few land in my books. Apparently, in retirement communities, *meeting at the sixteenth hole* on golf courses is code for secret hookups.

I love this place.

AFTER LUNCH with my favorite troublemakers, Grammy Jane and I head back to her house for a girly afternoon. It's our Christmas Eve tradition. We get into our matching Christmas-themed pajamas early, watch movies, and eat crap we don't normally allow ourselves to indulge in.

When the first movie ends and I'm in a chocolate fudge coma, she turns to me. "Are you ready to talk about him?" She crosses her arms in challenge. "If not, we can watch *G.I. Jane.*"

I roll my eyes. "Oh god, anything but that." Why the hell does she love that terrible movie?

She giggles, and I sigh. "I'm not sure what's left to say. Everything between us is good. It's great. He's sweet, loving, attentive, and more than outwardly into me. He practically lives to make my fantasies come true. I just can't go all in while I know he's lying to me. I'm enjoying him while I can. I imagine he has to go back to New York at some point."

"Where is he staying?"

I shrug. "I don't know. He always makes it a point to do things near my place so we never consider staying at his. He must think it's odd that I've never mentioned going to his place, but I don't want to force anything out of him. I'm still hoping he tells me the truth on his own."

"Tell me more about him."

I can't help the smile that finds my lips. "He's amazing. He's thoughtful and kind and treats me like I'm the center of his universe. I've never had a man look at me the way Trey DePaul does. The heat we share in the bedroom is like an inferno. I love that he's close to his sister. His niece and nephew are his happy place like you're mine."

She squeezes my hand in gratitude. "Has he met your boys?"

I shake my head. "No. Val and CJ know I'm seeing someone. That's it. I won't give them fake information, and obviously they'll know who he is the second they meet him."

"Perhaps he has a good reason. All I care about is that you're happy."

"He makes me happy. Sublimely happy. I just wish it wasn't so hard."

She lovingly rubs my back. "Just remember, life is like a penis."

I smile, loving that she brings levity to every situation. God knows what's about to come out of her mouth. "How so?"

"Sometimes it's up and sometimes it's down. But it won't be hard forever."

"How beautiful. Do you have a pillow with that sewn in?"

"No, but maybe I should get one."

I WAKE in the morning to the now familiar feeling of Trey's arms wrapped around my body from behind. I mindlessly trace the veins in his muscular forearms. I've never thought of myself as a forearm woman, but his arms drive me wild. They exude strength and power.

I'm ogling his arms when I look around and it occurs to me that I'm at my grandmother's house and Trey is in bed with me. *What the hell?*

I turn around in his arms, which causes him to stir. We're nose to nose when his eyes blink open and he smiles.

"Umm…what are you doing here?"

He moves my hair out of my face, and, in his sexy morning voice, croaks, "I missed you."

"I've been gone for one day."

He squeezes my body close to his and kisses my neck. "One day too long."

"How did you get in?"

"Grammy Jane loves me. We're besties."

He starts to move his lips toward mine, but I hold my hand up. "Morning breath."

"Don't care."

His lips take mine. I'm hesitant at first but then give in when his warm lips latch on. This feels bizarrely intimate.

His hands move up my sleep shorts and over my bare hips. I've noticed he loves to have his hands on my hips, and I more than enjoy it.

He pulls my top leg over him until I can feel his erection between my legs. He's always ready to go.

I mumble into his mouth, "What trope are we doing?"

He smiles into my mouth. "The madly in love trope."

"I don't think that's an official book trope."

He kisses along my jaw and whispers, "It's ours, baby."

This guy.

I feel around his body and discover that he's naked. Naked Trey is the sexiest thing in the world. His body is a dream. He's every book boyfriend I've ever created, rolled into one.

He easily maneuvers my pajamas off until I'm completely naked too. He moves his fingers between my legs. "You have no idea what a turn-on it is for me that you're always so wet."

"It's not just for you. It's all guys who do it for me."

He lifts his head in shock, and I giggle. "Sorry, it seemed cliché to say *it's all you*. I can't imagine I'm the first woman to make you hard."

"You're the first woman who incentivized me to put an extra hole in my dick."

I giggle again. "Fair enough." I gently run my fingers through his hair as my face turns serious. "No one has ever made me feel as good as you make me feel."

He nods. "That's much better."

We're about to take things up a notch when my bedroom door opens. Fortunately, we're covered by the blankets.

I lift my head to see Grammy Jane's smiling face. "Grammy Jane, what kind of grandmother allows a strange man to slip into her granddaughter's bed in the middle of the night? I'm appalled."

She looks around until her eyes find my pajamas on the floor. "You were so appalled that your pajamas fell off?"

I let out a laugh. "No, I blame Trey for that."

"If that man were in my bed, my pajamas would suddenly fall off too. They almost fell off from one room over."

Trey grins widely. "You two are so cute together. Merry Christmas to you both." He reaches over to his bag on the floor and pulls out two small gifts. He hands one to me and one to Grammy Jane.

I whine, "Ugh, Trey, I didn't bring your gift with me."

"Waking up to two beautiful ladies is my gift. Open them."

Mine is a long, rectangular-shaped gift and Grammy Jane's is a small square one. We both tear at our respective wrapped gifts. I open a velvet box and gasp. It's a stunning emerald bracelet. "Trey, this is too much."

"It's the same color as your eyes. I saw it and immediately thought of you."

Grammy Jane opens hers and it's the matching stud earrings. Her face furrows. "Trey, I can't accept this."

"They match your eyes too. One day, you can pass them along to Gemma and the set will be reunited. For now, enjoy them."

Grammy Jane deadpans, "He's been here for a few hours and he's already killing me off."

Trey and I both laugh.

She looks at Trey. "I have everything you asked for. Come out when you two are…ready."

At that, she walks out the door and closes it behind her.

I look at him in question. "What was that about?"

"I gave her some ingredients that I need to make you ladies Christmas breakfast and other fun treats. We can make everything together."

My shoulders fall. "I hate that you're missing this tradition with your family. I know it means a lot to you."

He softly kisses my lips. "I hope it becomes *our* tradition."

I get a knot in my throat. I'm so confused by him.

Before I can respond, he nods toward the bracelet. "May I?"

I hold out my wrist. "Thank you. It's beautiful."

"It pales in comparison to your beauty."

He clasps the truly stunning piece of jewelry around my wrist and rubs his thumb over it. "I love it on you. There are more pieces in the collection."

"I don't need you to buy me things. I just want you. The *real* you."

I do my best to emphasize the word real, hoping he'll confess, but he doesn't. He simply suggests we get dressed and get started on breakfast.

We're now at the big Christmas Day pool party. Santa is doing his best to bounce around, even though I think he's nearing ninety-five at this point. It's been the same man playing Santa for as long as my grandmother has lived here.

Every single elderly woman here has danced with Trey in his adorable Santa hat. Somehow, he makes Santa sexy, something I never thought I'd consider. I suddenly want to do him in nothing but that hat.

He's happily indulged the enamored women of this community, and he happens to be an amazing dancer.

I look around. Despite the warm temperature, this place truly embodies the Christmas spirit. Not only did the community spare no expense when it came to their Christmas décor, but it's full of smiles and holiday cheer.

I can't help but laugh to myself at the line of women waiting to dance with my man. Apparently when my grandmother learned late last night that Trey was flying in, she told her friends not to acknowledge who he is. Half the people in this community are originally from New York. All of them would have known right away but are playing along.

We had such a fun morning cooking together. He's shockingly talented in the kitchen. The french toast was the best I've ever had in my life. And then we made Christmas cookies. He was such a natural at it, clearly taking joy in working in the kitchen and in spending time with me.

He fed me, doted on me, touched me, kissed me, and loved me. It's truly like a dream. One I'm afraid will morph into a nightmare.

Grammy Jane stands next to me as we watch Trey twirl Happy around the poolside dance floor with a huge smile on his face, though not as big as the one on Happy's face.

She rubs my arm. "He's wonderful."

"I know."

"He's in love with you."

"I know."

"You're falling in love with him."

I close my eyes. "I know. I don't understand. It's all happened so quickly."

"I knew the moment I met your grandfather. When it's the right one, you know."

"But he's still lying to me about who he is."

"I suspect he has his reasons. I think it's time to confront him. I'd say you need to do so before you get in too deep, but you're already there, sweetheart."

I nod. "You're right."

I walk over to Trey and Happy. "You're monopolizing my man. May I cut in?"

Happy scowls but reluctantly pulls away. Trey happily takes me into his big arms. I wrap my arms around his neck and look up at him.

He smiles down at me. "Finally, the woman I want to dance with."

"Happy might murder me in my sleep to get to you."

He chuckles. "She kept grabbing my ass."

"I bet she did."

"She told me the funniest joke."

"She's full of them. What was it?"

"What did one saggy boob say to the other saggy boob?"

"What?"

"If we don't get some support soon, people will think we're nuts."

I let out a laugh. "Typical Happy joke."

I lift on my tippy toes and kiss his lips.

"What was that for?"

"Thank you for today. All of it. Your thoughtful gifts, the beautiful breakfast, and for being so good to my grandmother and her friends. You made this Christmas a special one."

"I'd do anything for you, Gemma."

How can a man look so sincere when I know he's hiding something?

He expertly twirls me a few times and I giggle. "Why are you such a good dancer?"

"My parents forced Diana and me to take lessons for years. They said it would look good on our college applications."

"But you didn't go to college, did you?"

He shakes his head.

I didn't mean to do it in this setting, but it slips out. "Because the Bombers drafted you right out of high school."

He stops moving and his smile immediately fades away. He's

quiet for a few long beats before asking, "How long have you known?"

"Since you tapped on my shoulder at the bar, and I turned around and saw you."

He exhales a long breath, almost as if a burden has been lifted. "Can we go for a walk and talk about it?"

I nod.

I motion to my grandmother that we're leaving, and we exit the pool area. Given the time of year, it already gets dark before five o'clock. We walk away from the bright lights of the party into the twilight.

He takes my hand in his and I let him. "Well, you haven't kicked me in the balls or thrown me out, so I suppose that's a good sign. I don't want to have a third-act breakup."

I roll my eyes. "This isn't a romance novel, Trey. I'm not interested in throwing a dramatic tantrum about betrayal and storming off where we both wallow in misery for weeks or months. I want an honest conversation. It's all I've ever wanted from you. I need to understand why. Why have you been lying to me for two months? You can't tell me you love me and then also lie to my face every single day. The two things simply don't go hand in hand."

"Gemma, besides my last name and job, everything I've said to you is the truth."

"You live in Philadelphia?" I accusatorily ask.

He winces knowing there's more to it than his name and job. "You know I don't."

"Where have you been staying?"

"With my friend Layton."

My eyes nearly pop out of my head. "As in Layton Lancaster?" Only the biggest baseball star on the planet.

He nods. "Yes, he's one of my best friends."

"Start talking, *DePaul.*"

"Cheetah—"

"As in Cruz Gonzales?" Another huge baseball star.

"Yes, he's also a close friend. I was out to dinner in New York City with Layton, Cheetah, and our agent, Tanner Montgomery. Tanner just got divorced, and we were all trying to cheer him up. Cheetah kept looking at his phone. It turns out that he was watching your Book Boyfriend Builders video."

Fucking hell, that video had a far reach. Famous baseball players? Our drunk asses were crazy.

He continues. "He's a romance book reader so he knew who all of you were."

"Cheetah Gonzales, the famous baseball player, reads our books?"

"Yes. Religiously. He turned the phone to show us the video, and I swear to god, it was like a shot to the heart when I saw your face. You were the most beautiful woman I had ever seen in my life. Your laugh and smile were intoxicating. I couldn't take my eyes off you. There was nothing I wouldn't do to meet you. I didn't think. We sat right there at dinner and filled out the application."

"You're telling me that Layton Lancaster, Cheetah Gonzales, and Tanner Montgomery all sat there with you to fill out our Book Boyfriend application?"

He nods. "Yes. We all contributed something to it."

"What about—"

"I wrote the personal statement myself. Cheetah took the picture of my ass. That was his idea. The personal statement was all me."

I nod. "Why lie about who you are?"

"I didn't want to use my notoriety. You have no idea what it's like to never know a woman's true intentions. They see money and fame before us as individuals."

"And once we met?"

"I wanted you to get to know me, Trey, the man who was already head over heels for you. Not Trey DePaul the baseball player."

I sigh. Part of me understands it, and part of me is still hurt.

"Everything I've told you since is true. There was no Jenna. I made her up to get to know you and spend time with you."

"How could you possibly think that I wouldn't recognize you?"

"I'm not Layton, with paparazzi following me wherever I go. People in New York know me, but I'm not known everywhere. I don't have issues like he has all over the country." He rubs his beard. "Plus, I have this now. I'm not allowed to grow it during the season. I thought I could fly under the radar for a bit."

"You know I'm into sports."

"Football, not baseball. You've never once mentioned baseball."

"Because baseball isn't in season right now."

He shrugs.

"When were you going to tell me?"

"Cheetah begged me to tell you. I tried so many times, but something would always happen that would make me afraid. I decided I wanted you to fall in love with me first." His eyes fill with tears. "So you wouldn't leave me. But it was becoming too much to bear. I was truly planning to tell you when you got home from Florida. Then you left yesterday morning, and I missed you. I couldn't go the week without you."

I take a few deep breaths. I don't know what to do.

He falls down to his knees in front of me, buries his face in my stomach, and wraps his arms around me. "I love you. I'm willing to do anything to make this right." He looks up at me. "Tell me what I can do."

I look down at him and run my fingers through his wavy hair. "What happens when you go back to New York? It's not like you have a regular job where we can see each other on the weekends. You play every weekend."

He visibly swallows. "Would you consider moving to New York? Moving in with me?"

My whole body freezes. Shock isn't a big enough word to describe how I'm feeling right now.

"Trey, we've known each other for two months. We've been dating for a few weeks. I'm expected to uproot my entire life? I own a house. I have a job that I love. I'm not even bar-certified in New York. I have friends. Friends you've never even met, and I haven't met yours. I have a life in Philly. One that makes me happy. And I'm not over the fact that you lied to me. That will never be okay for me."

His face falls, visibly in pain. "I promise to never lie again." Tears fall down his cheeks. "Please consider it."

"No, not right now. I think you should go home, Trey." I hold up my hands before he protests. "I'm not ending things, but I need some time to process."

"I'm afraid if I leave, I won't see you again."

The pain in his eyes is nearly unbearable.

"I promise that's not the case. I told you we'd spend New Year's Eve together. I want to bring my friends for you to meet, and I want to meet yours."

He nods. "Okay. I'll call them." He licks his lips nervously. "Do you want me to leave tonight?"

I shake my head. "I'm not kicking you to the curb on Christmas. It can wait until tomorrow."

He stands, and we walk back to my grandmother's house in silence with him practically glued to me. Once inside, he immediately goes to the bathroom followed shortly thereafter by the sounds of the shower running.

My mind is a clusterfuck of emotions, but I know I don't want him to leave feeling sad and uncertain, and I don't want to ruin his Christmas. He gave up being with his family to be with me. He was amazing with everyone today. All of that means something.

I remove my bathing suit and coverup before quietly stepping into the shower behind him. I rub my hands over his broad back. He jerks in surprise before turning around. I look him up and down. He truly is a beautiful man.

Without any words, he takes me into his arms and brings his

lips to mine. I love the way he tastes and the way he kisses me. How has it become so familiar and comfortable in such a short time?

He lifts me, and I wrap my legs around him. We kiss for several long minutes as if it could be our last. It's obviously in the back of both of our minds.

He presses me against the tile wall and kisses down my body until he reaches my nipple. It hardens at the feel of his warm tongue as he ravishes my breasts for minutes on end.

I moan, "Trey. Get inside me."

Without any hesitation, he swivels his hips and slips inside me. My jaw falls slack. It feels so fucking good. Every. Damn. Time.

He mumbles into my neck. "Tell me you feel how special this is. We're special."

I know he's right. We *are* special. I can't deny it. Despite the madness of how we got together and the lie that's been here the whole time, the chemistry and connection we share are undeniable.

He begins slow, purposeful movements inside my body as he peppers kisses over my jawline. "I love you so much. That's real. Don't ever doubt it."

I cover his mouth with my hand. "No more words." I can't deal with them. "Don't tell me how you feel, Trey. Show me."

His lips take mine again as he manages to beautifully make love to me against the tile wall of my grandmother's shower.

When it's over, we clutch each other in silence until the water runs cold.

Twelve

THE LONGEST FIVE days of my life. These have been the longest five days of my life. Every time my phone rang, I feared it was her calling to end things.

I'm pretty sure I have an ally in her grandmother. That's been my only saving grace. She pulled me aside before I left and told me she was confident things would work out between us. I'm praying she's right.

I'm in an Uber on the way to a club with Layton, Cheetah, and their teammate Ezra Decker. He's a friend of theirs. I've only met him a handful of times. He seems like a good guy.

Cheetah asks, "Are Gemma's friends as hot as her?" She and a bunch of her friends are meeting us there for a New Year's Eve party.

I glare at him with a disapproving scowl on my face. "Val, CJ, and Taylor are off-limits. They're her close friends, and I don't need you fucking them and leaving them, causing years of issues for Gemma and me. Taylor is bringing two friends who I know Gemma doesn't consider her friends. You can fuck them."

He twists his lips. "What do they look like?"

"I have no idea. I haven't met any of her friends. I know Val and CJ have been her closest friends since they were kids, and Taylor since college. That's it."

Layton shrugs as if he doesn't have a care in the world. He always goes home with a woman. He barely has to work for it. Cheetah does too, but for some reason, he enjoys a bit of a chase.

We walk into the club and are immediately escorted by management to the VIP area. We have a huge roped-off booth big enough for the ten of us. There are several bottles of good champagne on ice waiting for us when we arrive, along with bottles of vodka and whiskey. Yep, sometimes it's good to be a baseball player.

We sit in the booth and enjoy our first round as we wait for our guests. I'm truly on edge. I have no idea how things are going to play out.

Layton grabs my shaking knee. "Fuck's sake, man. Chill out. It will all work out in the end."

"One day you'll meet the right woman and lose all your chill. I'm buying a front-row ticket."

Ezra chuckles. "I'm not sure that will ever happen. Too many women have been *#laidbylayton*."

Layton gives a cocky smirk.

Cheetah places his hand on my shoulder. "Don't freak out, but Gemma is headed this way with two good-looking guys."

I immediately turn toward the VIP area entrance where I see her in a form-fitting, short red dress that leaves little to the imagination though somehow, it's still elegant. It's got a low neckline, and her full tits look amazing. Her hair is in a stylish ponytail, and her lips are painted her signature red.

He sucks in a breath. "Fuck, DePaul, she's so hot. Her body is ridiculous. You're a lucky man."

My mouth waters, but he's right. She's flanked on either side by two tall guys, a brunette and a blond. Her arms are linked through theirs and they're all laughing. What the fuck?

I practically sprint from my seat to her. She gives me the sexiest smile when I approach.

I grab her into my arms and lift her off the ground as I kiss the shit out of her. She lets out a small screech at first but then runs her fingers through my hair and kisses me right back. Deeply. She even moans.

Take that, fuckers.

She smiles into my mouth. "I missed you too." She pats my arm. "Now put me down."

I begrudgingly place her feet on the ground but tuck her snugly into my side. *Very* snugly.

The brunette guy chuckles. "I think someone wants everyone to know you're his."

I practically bark, "Who are you?"

He holds out his hand with an unaffected smile. "I'm Valentino Mancini. My friends call me Val. I hear you have a magical dick."

Gemma punches his arm. "Where's your bro code?"

I pinch my eyebrows together. "*You're* Val? Gemma's best friend Val?"

He chuckles. "She didn't tell you that her best friends are men, did she? Classic Gemma."

She shrugs. "I don't see you as men. You're sexless to me. If you didn't bang all my sorority sisters when you guys visited me in college, I wouldn't be sure either of you had a penis."

The blond lets out a laugh as he holds out his hand. "I'm Christopher Johns. Everyone calls me CJ. And to be clear, I have a penis." He leans forward and loudly whispers, "And it's really big."

Gemma gently kicks his shin. "No way it's big. Your hands are tiny."

He narrows his eyes at her. "That's a myth. Hand size means nothing."

She grabs my hand, which is admittedly unusually large, and holds it up in front of them. "Let me assure you, not a myth. He's got the biggest...hands, I've ever seen."

She bats her eyelashes at them.

I feel like I'm in the *Twilight Zone*, but I hear Cheetah, Layton, and Ezra all laughing behind me. Val laughs too before offering to buy drinks for everyone.

I shake my head. "We already have a few bottles at the table." I motion toward the booth. "Come join us."

They walk toward the booth, but Gemma pulls me to stay put. She wraps her arms around my waist and looks up at me with nothing but warmth in her eyes. "I missed you. How about a fresh start for us?"

I breathe a sigh of relief. "Yes. Please."

"No more lies."

I agree, "No more lies."

She squeezes me. "I missed your big hands on my body."

I run them over her ass and hips. "How about I keep them on you all night long to make up for lost time?"

She smiles. "I'd like that." Moving her hands up to my neck, she pulls me down and mumbles, "Lips too."

Her soft lips meet mine. I can taste vodka on her breath, but she seems happy, so I am too.

After breaking the kiss, I ask, "Did you start drinking without me?"

"We did a few shots before we came. We're ready for a good time."

"I didn't know that your two best friends were men."

She blows out a breath. "I guess I didn't mention it. Sorry. Honestly, it's no different for me than if they were women."

I'm trying to play it cool. "When you walked in, I thought you were trying to get me to do the why choose trope."

She lets out a laugh. "If I did, it definitely wouldn't be with those two." She makes a look of disgust. "Ugh. Gross."

I suppose that makes me feel better.

We walk over to the table. I sit and pull her onto my lap. She happily obliges.

Layton holds out his hand. "I'm Layton, it's nice to finally meet you."

Gemma proceeds to do the whole long handshake routine that he does with their coach on the field.

He smiles at her. "I love that you know our handshake."

She giggles. "I'm a big fan. I love watching you guys play. CJ, Val, and I go to a bunch of games every year. A few more drinks, and I'm going to ask you to record a video for my grandmother. She's obsessed with you."

"Any time. Trey said that Grammy Jane is a riot."

She looks at me and tilts her head. "You told Layton Lancaster about Grammy Jane?"

"Of course. She's the best, and she means a lot to you."

She traces my lower lip with her index finger. "Remind me to tell you something later when we're alone."

"Okay."

She then holds out her hand for Cheetah. "Nice to meet you too. I love it when you dance on the field."

He winks at her. "I love it when you watch me dance. You'll have to join me on the field this year. Maybe we'll do a slow dance together."

I squeeze her possessively. "Don't flirt with my girl, dickhead."

"Can't help it. She's smokin' hot."

Gemma smiles. "You're a troublemaker, Cheetah, aren't you?"

He grins as he nods. He loves pushing buttons.

"I hear you're a romance reader."

He looks around. "Shh. I have a rep to protect, but you're my dirty-talking queen. And I love all the fun places where your characters have sex. Have you done them in real life?"

Val and CJ simultaneously answer, "No."

How would they know?

She narrows her eyes at them. "You fuckers don't know everything about me. I've got a scene in an upcoming book that Trey will recognize. He bent me over my—"

I cover her mouth while Layton and Cheetah chuckle.

Cheetah asks, "How about you and I create a book club? We can have monthly meetings and chat about our favorite romance books."

She nods enthusiastically as she downs an entire glass of champagne. "I'd love that."

I whisper, "Slow down."

"Lighten up, Trey." She leans back into my body. "Drink up and take advantage of me. I'm feeling very frisky tonight."

With a tone of disbelief, CJ asks, "Did you really get your dick pierced for her?"

I nod. "I sure did. I'd do anything for her."

Layton lets out a laugh. "Cheetah and I went with him. We both passed out cold. It was nuts. Pun intended."

Gemma's eyes flutter. "Sooo fucking worth it."

Everyone laughs. Gemma is definitely in a good mood tonight. I wasn't sure what to expect, but it wasn't this. I suppose I should be happy.

I smirk. "I took the jewelry out for the first time the other day and the craziest thing happened. When I pissed, it came out of both holes."

Cheetah spits his drink. "Are you serious?"

"Yep. I looked it up. It appears as though I'm going to be a messy pisser for life."

They're all laughing. I knew they'd get a kick out of it.

I look around. "Is Taylor a guy too? I need to prepare myself."

I see Val and CJ's faces scrunch up. I guess they don't like Taylor.

Val answers, "No, she's a snobby girl, and her friends are even snobbier."

Gemma slaps his hand. "Stop it. Taylor is sweet. But, yeah,

her friends suck. I hate going out with them. They're manhunters."

Cheetah shrugs. "Are they hot?"

CJ nods. "Yes, it's their only redeeming quality."

Everyone at the table happily chats for a while until Gemma whispers in my ear, "Let's dance. I want to see your moves again."

That's not a bad idea. I joke, "Is this just an excuse to touch me?"

Her eyes light up. "Maybe."

We get up to go to the dance floor when Val pulls me aside and quietly says, "I watered down her vodka. I always do. She didn't drink that much. She's just nervous about the two of you. She's into you. *Really* into you, and it's scaring her."

I slap his back. "Thanks, man. I appreciate it."

He grabs my arm a little harder and gives me a look of warning. "Take care of our girl. She's a diamond."

I'm realizing how much these guys care about her. They look out for her. I think I like that.

I nod my head once. "Always."

We make our way to the crowded dance floor. We're out there having the time of our lives. We laugh and kiss, dance and touch, smile and fall more in love. She doesn't drink anymore. She's simply high on life and us.

At some point, the rest of the gang joins us, but Gemma and I are in our bubble. I barely register meeting Taylor and the two girls whose names I never caught. Layton and Cheetah end up dirty dancing with them.

Midnight rolls around, and I hold my girl tight in my arms as the clock ticks down to midnight. We stare into each other's eyes, and I know without any doubt that I will be looking into these same green eyes every New Year's Eve for the rest of my life. The look she's giving me suggests she feels the same.

Val and CJ eventually leave with two women they met. They first make sure that I'm taking care of Gemma.

It's nearly three in the morning when we crash through Gemma's front door kissing. She kicks off her shoes and throws her purse. She then whispers into my mouth, "Oh god, Trey, I want you so bad."

While still kissing her, I remove my blazer and toss it to the side somewhere. I mumble into her, "Longest five days of my life. This fucking dress gave me a perma-boner all night. I need to sink myself inside you. Stat."

She giggles. "Perma-boner. I like that expression. I'm using it in a book."

I break our kiss enough to lift her dress over her head. My eyes move up and down her body. She's in a red lace thong and matching strapless bra. I look at her in awe. She's so fucking hot. I have to grab my dick before he explodes.

She notices and licks her lips. "I need to suck your big dick. Pull it out. Right here."

"Let's go to your bedroom."

"No, right now. I need it. I want to choke on you."

At a speed I didn't know I was capable of, I unbutton and unzip my pants, freeing my straining cock.

As it springs free, she stares at it and declares, "You have the best dick," before dropping to her knees in front of me. She grabs the base while sucking my balls into her hot little mouth.

I hiss in pleasure.

After lavishing attention over every inch of my balls, she licks her way up and circles my piercing, flicking her tongue over it several times. This piercing may be the second-best decision I've ever made in my life. The first is applying to Book Boyfriend Builders.

I unbutton my shirt while she continues to pay glorious attention to my piercing. My dick is impossibly hard right now.

I look down, and we make eye contact. I command, "Open wide, baby," as she spreads her lips and feeds my cock into her mouth. I love watching it disappear between her full lips with her green eyes looking up at me.

Her head begins to bob up and down, never breaking that eye contact. This is the exact image that was playing in my mind when I got the piercing. It's so erotic to see it come to life like this. This woman is my every fantasy come to life.

"Touch your pussy, baby. Then show me how wet you are. I want to see how wet sucking my cock makes you."

Without hesitation, she slides her free hand into her panties and runs it through herself a few times before lifting her hand, showing me the evidence of her extreme arousal.

"Soaked. Like I thought." I grab her hand and suck her fingers into my mouth. "Hmm. Tasty. I've missed my favorite meal."

Her eyes shade over with lust as she stares up at me and moans on my dick. I can hear the sound of my piercing vibrating in the back of her throat.

She mumbles around me, "Fuck my mouth."

I grab onto her hair and thrust my hips a bit. Her eyes begin to water, but she takes every inch of me. This is the greatest sight I've ever seen. I can't hold off. "I'm about to blow."

She pulls back and pants, "I want it. Give it to me. Every drop."

Her mouth immediately latches on again. My whole fucking body tingles and goes numb as every ounce of blood travels to my cock. I let out a loud grunt as I come long and hard into her mouth. Like the goddess she is, she drinks every ounce of it.

When I'm done, I immediately lift her and smash my lips to hers. I can taste my saltiness on her.

After a deep kiss, she shoves my chest until we're standing a few inches apart and breathes, "I have a new trope I want you to try."

"Anything," I mutter, "except why choose."

She gives me a sexy smile. "Not why choose." She bites her lip. "Ever since I saw what a good dancer you are, I can't stop thinking of you stripping for me. I want the striptease trope."

I narrow my eyes at her. "Is that a real trope?"

She shrugs as she looks my body up and down. "It is now."

I smirk. "No problem." I pull out my phone from my pocket. "You have a song in mind, ma'am? I take requests."

She places her hands on her hips. "Only the greatest striptease song ever created from the greatest movie of all time. 'Pony' from *Magic Mike*."

I chuckle. "Of course. I should have known."

I pull it up on my phone and hit play as I begin swaying my hips to the sultry beat.

She stares at my movements with amusement sparkling in her eyes.

While still dancing, I slowly tease removing my shirt, but don't actually remove it just yet. It's complete with a few ab rolls and hip thrusts.

She watches on with rapt fascination as she bites her bottom lip and her fingers dip into her panties.

I turn around, bend at the waist, and then slowly make my way back up. With my back still facing her, I slide my pants down my legs, bending over again.

I hear her moans of pleasure. She whispers to herself, "Best ass ever."

After kicking my pants away, I slowly dance over to her, pick her up, and swing her around a bit. She squeals with delight before I lay her on the ground.

Maintaining an arm's length distance as I hover above her, I roll my body and gyrate over her just like the guys do in the movie, teasing but not yet touching any part of her body. I suck her Gemma-soaked fingers into my mouth all without breaking stride.

She writhes and breathes, "You're so hot."

I barely brush my covered cock across her covered pussy

each time I roll my hips over her. Her eyes flutter with each pass and she attempts to thrust her hips up, desperate for contact.

Looking around the room, I notice a Santa hat hanging on her Christmas tree. I stand and quickly grab it before placing it on my head.

She reaches her hands toward me. "I want Santa inside my chimney."

I wiggle my eyebrows. "Ho, ho, ho, down your chimney I go."

She giggles. I love that sound.

Standing over her, I slowly remove my shirt, making a teasing spectacle of it, much to her delight. She has her hands behind her head as she watches on with a huge smile on her gorgeous face.

After discarding my boxer briefs, I then repeat the gyrating routine over her again. She reaches up for my cock and begins stroking it.

My body hovers and ripples over hers until the song ends. She tosses the Santa hat and mouths, "Fuck me. Now."

Easily lifting her off the ground, I carry her to her bedroom with her gorgeous body wrapped around mine. She kisses, licks, and nibbles my neck and shoulders along the way. She's bordering on out of control. I love it.

I fall onto the bed with her straddling me. After removing her bra, I run my hands over every inch of her body while she does the same to me. It's like we can't get enough of one another. We've both missed each other and are making up for lost time.

She grinds her hips over my erection while her nipples rub over my chest. This right here is what I've missed the most. The intimacy. The closeness to her. The feeling of her soft body on mine. In a relatively short time, it's become what I crave. Gemma Fairchild is my drug of choice, and I'm completely addicted.

She pulls at her thong and breathes, "Too much between us."

On autopilot, I easily rip them off her. She moans out, "Oh fuck, I love when you do that. Such a good book boyfriend."

I can feel the evidence of her statement dripping down over me.

She pushes my shoulders back and crawls up my body until she's sitting on my face. "I'm so turned on, Trey. Make me come. I want it."

I grab her ass and smash my entire face into her pussy, immediately sinking my tongue into her channel. She grabs fistfuls of my hair and basically fucks my tongue and my entire face.

I love how she owns her pleasure and takes what she needs. She's never a passive bystander in our lovemaking, even when I'm controlling the movements.

I rub my nose over her clit, which sends her into overdrive. "Oh god, this will be quick. I need it."

She grinds her hips on my tongue. I push it as far into her as humanly possible. She's totally worked up and screaming my name. I can feel her clench around me as she comes into my mouth.

I rub my entire face through her fluids and happily slurp them up. So good.

She slides down my body. Her come spreads down my chest and abs. Is it weird that I never want to clean it off? I wear it proudly.

Her saturated pussy is now resting on my hard cock. She licks across my chin. "Hmm. I love it when your dimple tastes like me."

"I get the appeal. Nothing tastes better than you. Now take what's yours. Grab my dick and take it home, baby."

She smiles into my face before lifting her body enough to wrap her delicate fingers around my cock. After bringing my tip to her entrance, she sinks down only an inch or two before lifting again.

She repeats the same process over and over, never sinking all the way down. I don't think I've ever had a woman do this to me. She teases both of us with just my pierced tip. It's shockingly good. The anticipation and buildup are hot as hell. Her eyes are practically in the back of her head as she works us both over.

I'm tempted to slam her down on me, but curiosity gets the best of me. I want to see how this plays out.

She grabs her tits and squeezes her nipples. Despite losing herself a bit in the pleasure, she maintains control as her wetness practically pours down onto me.

I'm committing this moment to memory. It's so erotic and perfect.

Sliding my thumb to her clit, I begin moving it in circles. "Oh yes, Trey. Like that. Oh fuck. So good."

I can feel her begin to clench over my tip. She's going to come from just the tip.

Suddenly, she shouts, "Thrust up into me. Hard."

I grab her hips and slam up. She yells out as her entire

body convulses, and she immediately comes, her juices drenching me.

She shakes as she rides out her pleasure until she eventually stills, with me finally buried all the way inside her. I can feel her pussy continuing to pulsate around my cock. She just blew my mind.

After several long breaths, she looks down at me with a sexy smile and wiggles on top of me. "You up for a little peach play, Santa? 'Tis the season."

I nod. "Nothing says Christmas cheer and a happy New Year like a little sodomy."

Her responding smile quickly fades into a moan when I grab her ass hard and thrust my hips. "I'm up for anything that makes you come the way you just came."

She reaches toward her night table and opens the drawer. Her tits dangle in my face and I bite one of her nipples. She screeches out and then giggles before bending her head and biting my nipple. Hard. Fuck if my cock doesn't leak a little from that.

I easily flip us over, pin her arms back, and push my cock as deep inside her as I can. Slowly, I move in and out of her, but unlike when she was in control, my thrusts are deep. *Very* deep.

"Do you want me this deep in your ass?"

Her eyes flutter. "Y...yes. I want it." She points toward the drawer. "Grab the fuchsia bottle."

I look over into the oversized drawer. What the fuck? There are like ten vibrators, a bunch of other toys I've never seen before, and several bottles, all in different colors.

I lift an eyebrow in question, and she shrugs. "What? It was a long drought before you came into my life. I have needs."

"Do you use all this stuff?"

She gives me a sexy smile. "I know a sex scene I write is good enough when I can't get through reading it without engaging in some self-love."

"Your barometer of a decent sex scene is whether or not you have to stop and masturbate while rereading it?"

She laughs and nods. "Yes. It's called the Gemmabation scale. I think it's part of the metric system."

I chuckle. "Yep. I think I've heard of it. Millimeters, centimeters, meters, kilometers, and Gemmameters. It all makes perfect sense."

She giggles as she nods in agreement.

I reach over and grab the fuchsia bottle. Her smile widens. "See, you understand the color fuchsia. One of my author friends had an...incident because she didn't understand my color system. I had to fib and ensure her that the fuchsia was front door lube and not back door. It was a whole thing."

"I'm not even gonna ask about that one."

She giggles again. "It's better you don't." She clenches around my cock. "Are you ready for the peach-play trope?"

"Ass-fucking is a trope too?"

She shrugs. "Everything is a trope these days."

I pull out and easily flip her over. Opening the fuchsia bottle, I squeeze the lube all over her ass and on my cock. I give myself a few pumps to spread it out and then rub it through her apple of an ass.

Giving it a loud spank, I expect a yelp, but she moans. I love how dirty she is. Gemma Fairchild is all elegance and class on the streets, and lewd and dirty in the sheets. Or, as I like to call it, perfection.

She lifts on all fours and wiggles that ass. "Put your dick in my ass and fuck me."

Holy hell.

I add a bit more lube to my fingers and slip them inside her back entrance to help prepare her for me.

"Hmm. Yes. More. I need more."

After a few pumps, I withdraw my fingers, bring my tip to her puckered hole, and begin to slide it in. "Oh, fuck, Gemma. It's so tight. I won't last long."

"My clit is already about to explode. Holy fuck, that piercing." She pants, "Deep. I want you deep."

I push all the way in, and she shouts, "Yes!"

I have to remain still as I take in the scene before me. I'm buried to the hilt in the ass of the sexiest woman alive. I'm officially the luckiest man in the world.

I reach around and find her clit. She wasn't wrong. It's completely swollen and throbbing. I can practically feel her pulse in it.

Rubbing it with my fingers, I begin my slow, deep thrusts in and out of her. She reaches back and claws at me until we establish a rhythm, climbing the ascent together.

She wasn't kidding, she likes it deep in her ass. It doesn't take long for us both to explode in ecstasy.

When it's over, we collapse in a breathless heap of sweat, oil, and fluids. Once our breathing evens out, we decide to take a quick shower to rinse off.

Afterward, we lay in bed, sated, and I hold her in my arms. "That was incredible."

She sleepily answers, "Umm hmm."

"Before you fall asleep, can you tell me where we are?"

She closes her eyes and smiles. "We're at my house. In my bed."

I tickle her side, and she giggles.

"You know what I mean, wise ass. You and me. Where do we stand?"

She blows out a long breath as her head rests comfortably on my chest. "We've got about seven weeks until you have to leave for spring training. And then the madness of your season begins. I just want to enjoy these seven weeks with you without drama and pressure. We're new, Trey. We're still getting to know each other. I'm not making a life decision right now. My life is in Philly. I'm not one of those women who abandon who they are for a man. If I moved right now, I'd be jobless and friendless, and you'd be gone most of the time. I'd end up resenting you. Let's see where the next seven weeks take us. We're in no rush to make permanent decisions about the future."

I can't deny that I'm disappointed, but also can't deny the logic in what she's saying.

"I understand."

She lifts her head as her eyes meet mine. "You're upset."

"What do you want me to say? I'm in love with you. I want forever with you, but I'll always want you to be happy. I guess we'll see how it plays out."

She cups my cheek. "I'm falling in love with you. That's what I wanted to tell you earlier tonight. But I won't lose myself in us. It's not who I am. I've worked too hard to fall into that cliché."

I nod and kiss her head. "I understand. I really do."

After a few minutes, her breathing evens out and she's fast asleep on my chest. I have trouble falling asleep though. For the first time since I laid eyes on her in that video, I'm not sure if we are going to end up together.

I WAKE in the morning to a noise in the kitchen. Gemma is still fast asleep on my chest. Who's here?

I look around and realize I left all my clothes on the floor of her foyer. Gently slipping out of bed, I find a towel and wrap it around my waist.

I walk into the kitchen and see Val cutting up fruit. He turns and smiles when he sees me. "Good morning. Happy New Year."

"Umm, same to you. What are you doing here?"

"Unless Gemma stays in Florida, we always do brunch and watch football on New Year's Day. Since we were little kids. I brought all the bagels and stuff. CJ will be here shortly with the ingredients for mimosas. Gemma insists on that instead of beer on this one day each year, and we indulge her."

"You guys have a…unique relationship."

He shrugs. "I suppose. It's all we've ever known."

"And it's never been—"

"Never. Not once." He stops cutting the fruit and turns to look me in the eyes. "Look man, I'm not blind. I know Gemma is drop-dead gorgeous, but that's just not how it is between all of us. It's so fucking annoying how much society over-sexualizes men's and women's friendships. Do gay men not have male friends? Do gay women not have female friends? Gemma is no different than a sister. None of us would ever do anything to jeopardize the bond. She's had boyfriends in the past who got jealous, and she immediately cut them loose. Man to man, I'm telling you that we are the best of friends. We will *always* be in each other's lives. If you're too fucking insecure to manage it, then walk away. If you love her the way I think you do, then you might want to become friends with us too. We're pretty fucking awesome, and we would both happily take a bullet for her. You should be happy she has friends who love her the way we do."

I'm processing what he said when Gemma walks out in nothing but one of my T-shirts that I must have left here. Her nipples are practically poking through, and her long legs are on display.

She smiles when she sees me, wraps her arms around my neck, and pulls my head down for a kiss. "Hmm. Morning, sexy. Every hole in my body is sore."

My eyes widen and I nod toward Val, who just chuckles.

She rolls her eyes and loudly whispers, "He knows we had sex last night. It's not a secret."

Val turns his head to her. "How was it?"

She answers with a moan before saying, "In-fucking-credible. I came so many times."

Val winks at me before saying, "I had some pretty in-fucking-credible sex myself."

He and Gemma high-five.

I can only shake my head. "You all have a weird relationship."

They both laugh, and then Gemma sighs. "Wait until CJ gets here. He's the biggest freak of all of us."

We spend the day eating food and watching football. Seeing the three of them interact in such a familiar, casual way, oddly puts me at ease. And Val and CJ are, in fact, awesome guys.

CHAPTER

Thirteen

GEMMA

"OH GOD, YES. DON'T STOP."

I cling to Trey as his body moves inside mine for what we both know will be the last time for a long time.

He whispers into my lips, "I'm going to miss you. I love you."

I whisper back, "I love you too," before our lips lock again.

Yep, I've completely fallen in love with Trey DePaul. We haven't spent a single night apart in the past seven weeks. Almost all the evenings have been at my house in Philly, but I took the past few days off and am at his place in New York City. It's a magnificent penthouse overlooking Central Park. It looks like it belongs in a movie.

He needed to come home to pack before he flies to Florida for a month of spring training, the unofficial kickoff of his season. We've ambiguously agreed to see each other when we can throughout the season. New York City and Philly are only ninety minutes away from each other. He'll travel down during his one day off every other week, and when they have home games on the weekends, I plan to travel up. It's not ideal, but it will have to be our normal for the long, seven-month season.

We lay there in the aftermath, desperately clinging to each other. I rub my cheek on his now smooth face. He shaved last night per his team's requirements. "I love your scruff, but I equally love it when I can feel your soft face on mine."

He nuzzles into my neck. "I love everything about you."

Except that I won't move to New York for him. He doesn't need to say that out loud for me to know he's thinking it. We've had plenty of disagreements about this topic over the past seven weeks, but I'm not budging. We're still relatively new. I'm not making any rash decisions. Yet.

I've been to his place a small handful of times throughout the past two months. I noticed on this trip up here that he's made some changes. He cleared out the second closet in his bedroom. He also filled the second vanity and shower in the bathroom with duplicates of all the shampoos, conditioners, lotions, and just about every product that I use. All are color-coded to my specifications.

His alarm begins to ring, and he squeezes me tight. "I don't want to leave you."

I run my fingers through his hair and try to savor the feel of his naked body on mine. I breathe, "I know. Trey, if things…feelings change for you, I need you to be upfront with me. Separations sometimes change things. I know women must throw themselves at you all the time."

He lifts his head and looks at me like I've got three eyes. "Have you not heard a single word I've said to you in the past few months? There is no one else. There never will be. I'm in love with you. We're end game. When the logistics finally work out, we're getting married. I don't care how long I have to wait."

Tears sting my eyes. I'm left without words, so I simply nod.

He wiggles his dick over me. "Besides, you've marked me as yours."

I smile through my unshed tears. My Christmas gift to him was replacement jewelry for his dick piercing. It now has a "G" charm on it.

I joke, "You could always find a guy named Gary. That could work too."

He tickles me and we both laugh, trying to stuff down the emotions of our impending separation.

THREE WEEKS Later

"Knock, knock."

I look up from my office desk and see Darian and her husband, Jackson, at the door. He's got his arms around her from behind. He's constantly touching her. I always thought they had this magical, fairytale of a relationship. One that *normal* people don't have. It turns out that it can happen. Trey treats me the way Jackson treats Darian. Trey loves me the way Jackson loves her. Special, all-encompassing love does exist beyond the pages of romance novels.

I try to plaster a fake smile on my face. "Are you two headed out for the day?"

She nods. "We are. Reagan and Carter are picking us up for dinner." Reagan is her daughter and Carter is her son-in-law. "I just wanted to check on you before we leave."

"I'm fine. The Morton deal went through today. I'm finalizing the paperwork."

"I don't mean work, Gemma. I know the past few weeks have been hard on you. You miss him. It's okay to admit it."

I pinch my lips together and nod. "Only a little over a week until he's back in New York. I'm sure the partners of all baseball players miss their men."

"I'm not worried about them. I'm worried about you. Listen,

Jackson and I have talked about it. He does a lot of real estate deals in New York City. He'd welcome in-house counsel. If you want to move, I'll understand. There's a job waiting there for you."

I look up at Jackson. "You'd hire me?"

He smiles at me. "For Darian's tenth favorite employee? Of course."

We all laugh at the ongoing joke.

"I appreciate the offer. Can I think about it? I've never seen myself living anywhere but Philly, and I've never seen myself as the kind of woman who would uproot everything in her life for a man."

Darian gives me a small smile. "You're in love, sweetheart. It's okay to change course. Love changes you, and there's no shame in that. It's well worth it. And of course you can think about it. It's an open-ended offer."

"Thank you. I might go visit my grandmother for the weekend, leaving tomorrow after work. Maybe I'll surprise Trey at his game on Saturday."

She only lives an hour from where he's playing this Saturday.

"Why don't you make it a long weekend? Call in sick tomorrow."

"You're literally my boss. You can't encourage me to lie and call in sick."

She giggles. "Happy employees are productive employees. How about you work on the plane ride, and we'll call it even?"

I smile at the best boss in the world. The one I can't imagine ever leaving. "Deal."

Just then, Reagan appears in my doorway. She's about my age and is beautiful, with blonde hair and blue eyes, but looks nothing like Darian. She and I have always gotten along well, both with a sarcastic, dry sense of humor.

She gives me her mischievous smile. "Well, well. If it isn't my mother's secret love child." She always cracks jokes about how much more I look like Darian than she does.

I grin widely. "Hey, *sis*. Did you bring me a belated holiday gift?"

"I did." She reaches into her purse and pretends to search for one before lifting out her middle finger, turning it upright, and flipping me off.

I let out a laugh. "Good one. What a coincidence. I got the same thing for you." I use my middle finger to simulate putting on my lipstick.

She wiggles her eyebrows. "I hear you're banging Trey DePaul. Nice pull."

I nod in agreement. "Yep. Mom and I pull all the hotties."

I wink at Jackson, and they all laugh.

I UBER to Grammy Jane's house by late morning. She's standing outside to greet me. I immediately fall into her comforting arms and start sobbing.

She rubs my hair in her special, motherly way. "It's going to be fine."

"What am I going to do? I swore I'd never change who I am for a man."

"You don't need to change who you are, Gemma Morgan. You're going to have to learn to be a little flexible."

"But—"

"I know what you're going to say. It's okay to give yourself permission to bend. Don't ever break, but bending is needed from time to time. Both in and out of the bedroom."

I break out in a smile before she grabs my hand and pulls me into her house. "Come get changed. We'll have lunch at the pool with my friends. They always put a smile on your face."

Thirty minutes later, we're poolside with Happy, Millie, and Mortimer. They've asked me a few questions about Trey before it slips out that he was here last week. I snap my head toward my grandmother at the unexpected news.

She scrunches her face. "He stopped by on his day off. You know their spring training isn't too far away."

"What did he want? He didn't mention it to me."

She rubs my hand. "Just to chat about you. He loves you. The separation is hard for him too."

Mortimer smiles. "He sure does. He loves you almost as much as I love my Millie."

Millie rolls her eyes. "Oh please. If something happens to me, all you'll need is a cook, a cleaner, and a prostitute."

I giggle. "Stop it, Millie. Mortimer loves you."

She winks at me. I know she's just joking with him.

I turn to Happy. "What about your love life? What happened with Samuel?"

Grammy Jane shakes her head. "He asked her to marry him, and she broke his heart."

I gasp. "Why?"

Happy shrugs. "We had no future."

"How come?"

"His name is Samuel Heiman. How could I ever marry a man with that name?"

I think for a moment and then start laughing. Hysterically laughing.

When I eventually calm down, I deadpan, "I think Happy Heiman is a perfectly lovely name."

She quips, "For a hooker. Nope. Not doing it. I told him we can still have hoochie coochie, I'm just not marrying him." She sighs. "But he wants all or nothing."

"Happy, why would you deny yourself this for a silly reason? You're only hurting yourself. You're being very foolishly inflex —"

I stop myself before I finish the sentence. They all lean back in their chairs in satisfaction, giving me knowing looks.

This was a rehearsed setup to show me the error of my ways. God, I love these people.

I know what I have to do. It starts with me being a little flexible. I can't imagine my life moving forward without Trey. It's time to put my preconceived notions aside. I need to move to New York to be with him. I've got a good job, a place to live, and Trey.

It's not far from Philly. I'll still see my friends. I'm suddenly feeling resolute on this.

We're going to his game tomorrow, but I don't think I'll tell him. I might move in secretly so I'm there when he arrives home next weekend. It will be his welcome home surprise. I can't wait.

GRAMMY JANE GOT us tickets right behind the Bombers' dugout. Spring training games are different from regular season games. The stadiums are much smaller. It's akin to the size of a college game.

We arrive early to catch their warmup routine. After making our way to the seats, I simply watch Trey looking sexy in his uniform as he prepares for the game. He hits, he fields, and, most importantly, he stretches. I could sit here all day watching him stretch. Was stretching always this erotic? He's so hot.

He hasn't seen us yet, but he's finally making his way toward the dugout. I'm about to yell his name when at least twenty-five grown women scream for him. I look around. What the hell? All these women are begging for his attention, shouting his name. He doesn't even bother to lift his head and acknowledge them. *Take that, bitches.*

I need to yell something that will grab his attention. "Hey, Demon Trey, know any good plumbers? I need my pipes unclogged."

He stops dead in his tracks and frantically scans the area we're sitting in until his eyes meet mine. The biggest grin I've ever seen breaks out on his handsome face. I can't help matching it with one of my own. God, I've missed him.

He leaps up onto the top of the dugout and then into the

stands. I think everyone around us is confused. Grammy Jane starts giggling.

He practically sprints to me, lifts me in his arms, and kisses the shit out of me. Everyone around us starts clapping and cheering but he doesn't care in the least. He dips me as he continues to ravish my mouth. Our tongues meet, and I, too, forget our audience.

After *several* long minutes, he pulls me back up as our lips break. His forehead remains pressed to mine, and his arms continue to hold me close.

Slightly out of breath from that epic kiss, he breathes, "What are you doing here?"

I smile as I run my fingers over his handsome face. "I missed my man."

He grabs my face and dots kisses all over it. "I've missed you so fucking much." His voice cracks. "This is hard."

I know at this moment that I'm doing the right thing. All my remaining doubts fade away. I can't wait for him to find out that I'm going to move to New York for him.

"I know. For me too."

I go to wipe my red lipstick from his mouth, but he grabs my wrist. "Don't. I want it on me."

I lean over and whisper, "If we can get a few minutes of privacy, I'll leave you a ring of that lipstick on your dick."

He sucks in a breath, throws me laughing over his shoulder, and starts running toward the locker room.

He yells back, "Sorry, Grammy Jane. I need her for ten minutes."

Grammy Jane shouts back, "Make it twenty."

TREY

I spent the best night with Gemma. Reconnecting with her was just what I needed. If I've learned anything over the past few weeks, it's that I can't be away from her.

After she leaves for the airport, I call Tanner. He answers right away. "Hey, buddy. Feeling better?"

He knows how much I've been missing my girl. We've had several conversations about it recently.

"I'm feeling more steadfast. Move forward with everything we discussed."

"You'll probably take a big PR and financial hit."

"Don't care. Make it happen. I'll handle things on my end."

Fourteen

GEMMA

IT'S FRIDAY, my last official day in the office I've called home for five years. I'm tying up as many loose ends as I can. I'll still work remotely for Darian for the next few months. My job with Jackson's company won't start until I feel like I'm leaving things in the right hands at the firm. When Trey has road trips, I'll come back to Philly and work here until everything is properly transitioned.

I've begun to box some of my belongings at my house. The move will have to be gradual. I couldn't manage everything at the office *and* packing in just a few days. I'm planning on my house going up on the market next month. I'm truly taking a leap of faith, but I know in my heart that Trey is *the one*. He's worth the upheaval to my life.

I look down at my phone when it buzzes with a text notification. It's my *Perverts* group chat.

I let out a laugh. God, I love my author chat group.

> Libby: You can't use the word pussy 87 times in the same book. You have to switch it up. Vagina, genitals, private parts, vag, lady bits, muff... Need I go on?

> Me: You know I'm partial to pink canoe.

> JoJo: Anything is better than moistened folds.

> Me: I throw the word moist into every single book just because people hate it. At least I amuse myself.

> JoJo: Ugh. I know. It's gross.

> Me: If we were British, we could write fanny, but we can't get away with that shit.

> Ava: Ooh. Fanny. I like that.

> Libby: I just used bajingo in a book. I was debating between that and fufu.

> Ava: I'll take your leftovers. Fufu for the win.

I smile as I place my phone on my desk. I love those clowns. They always bring a smile to my face. Every single day.

Darian suddenly runs into my office, completely out of breath. "Come to the conference room. Right now."

I quickly follow her into our big conference room. I assume they're having a goodbye party for me, but that's not what I find. Everyone in the office is sitting, looking up at the big-screen television that hangs on the wall.

It's tuned to ESPN. It appears to be some sort of news conference. There's a stage and podium.

I look closely at the three men sitting near the podium until the one on the left comes into focus. "Is that Trey?"

Darian nods. "It is."

The scroll bar underneath reads *Bombers to announce blockbuster trade at five p.m.* I glance down at my watch. It's four fifty-nine.

What's happening? Is it him? Where is he going?

Trey and the elderly Bombers' owner, George Stein, move to stand at the podium. George brings the microphone toward him.

"Good evening, everyone. Thanks for being here. Trey DePaul joined this team eleven years ago, right out of high school. He made an immediate impact on this organization both on and off the field. In addition to being a true team leader, he's among the most level-headed young men I've ever had the privilege to have play for me. When he came to me this week and requested a trade..."

He pauses as he becomes emotional and wipes his eyes with a tissue, but eventually continues.

"To say I was shocked is an understatement. When he explained his reasons, I had to respect them. They're for him to share, but effective immediately, the Bombers have traded Trey DePaul to the Philly Cougars for Jim McMichael, Jeremy Horns, and multiple draft picks which will be released to the press shortly."

He holds out his hand to Trey for him to shake, which he does.

"Son, we'll miss you, and we wish you well."

Trey nods as he stands and briefly hugs George. I see tears forming in his eyes as he adjusts the microphone up toward his mouth.

"Thank you, Mr. Stein."

He swallows, clearly equally filled with emotion.

"I moved to New York as a kid at eighteen with one duffle bag and without any friends or family in the area. The people of this city embraced me as one of their own and made me feel at home. Mr. Stein treated me with nothing but kindness and respect. I love this city and

the Bombers more than words can express, but there comes a time in a man's life when he has to make difficult choices."

He pauses, gathering himself. Tears begin streaming down my cheeks as my heart aches for him.

"Unfortunately, we live in a society where women are often asked—no, expected—to sacrifice their own needs for men. Women giving up careers and dreams has become the norm. Why is that?"

He wipes his eyes with a tissue. I wish I was there to hold his hand. To hold him. To tell him I love him for what he's about to do.

"I want to be honest with you all. I've found myself in love with a woman who lives in Philadelphia. Born and bred there. She's never considered living anywhere else. She has a career, family, friends, and a community she loves. I want to respect everything she's worked for. As much as I've always seen myself as a Bomber for life, I understand that I have a job different from most. Partners of baseball players don't have it easy. They're left alone for days and weeks at a time. Is it fair of me to ask her to move to a strange city only for me to be on the road for more than four months of the year? I don't think it is. After a great deal of self-reflection and thinking about my future and home, the answer was clear. She's my home. She's in Philly. I love the Bombers, I always will, but number eighteen is taking this show to Philly. Thank you, New York. You'll always have a small piece of my heart, but my girl has the rest of it."

He steps aside and some other man takes the podium. I think it's Trey's agent, but I'm not sure. I can't hear anything over the pounding in my heart. It's so loud it's drowning out the whispers and chatter in the conference room.

All eyes in the room are on me as tears stream down my cheeks. I'm left speechless by what he just did.

I hear my name and turn toward the door. Grammy Jane is standing there with Val and CJ.

My eyebrows pinch together. "What are you all doing here?"

Trey emerges from behind them. "I invited them."

I breathe, "Trey." I point to the television. "How…how are you—"

"We recorded it two hours ago. I wanted to be here when you found out."

Emotions overcome me as I croak out, "You didn't have to do this. I was planning to move. I was going to surprise you this weekend."

He shakes his head. "I've been thinking about it for a while. I meant every word I said. *I* should be the one to move, not you."

In tandem, we glide toward each other, and he takes me into his arms. Tears pour down both our cheeks.

I look toward my grandmother and two best friends who are all smiling like fools.

Trey answers my unspoken question. "I wanted them here for this."

"For wh—"

Before I can get out the words, he drops down on one knee and opens a box with an exceedingly large diamond ring sitting inside.

"Gemma, you know full well that I caught an incurable case of insta-love the second I laid eyes on you."

I smile at him continuing to refer to it like a disease.

"After spending time with you, I knew my instincts were right. You and I are meant to be. When I close my eyes and imagine my future, I not only see you in it. You *are* it. I want—no, I *beg*—you to spend your life with me. Let me love you every single day. Marry me." He nods toward the television. "There are no more obstacles standing in our way. It can be you and me living here in Philly. Your home. Our home."

I twist my lips. "Now I sort of feel compelled to say yes since you just changed the paths of two billion-dollar franchises for me."

He smiles, knowing that I'm only joking with him.

I wipe the tears covering my face. "I can't believe you did this for me."

"For us. I did it for us." He gives me his adorable smile. "You once said that every good romantic comedy ends with a grand romantic gesture. I suppose this was mine."

I shake my head and grab his face with my hands. "No, my love, this isn't our ending. It's our beginning."

I hold out my left hand, and, with a huge grin, he places the ring on my finger. He then stands, lifts me into his arms, and kisses the hell out of me to a sea of cheers.

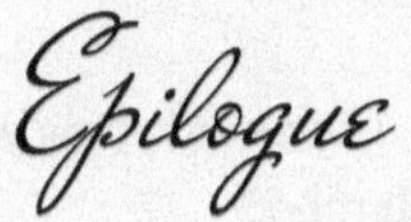

Epilogue

GEMMA

I LEAN BACK on the couch with a full belly. Pointing to the television, I instruct Val, "Flip to Trey's game."

He shakes his head. "Nope. Not happening. Not a good idea, and Trey has forbidden us from doing so."

My shoulders fall. "Ugh. Is it that bad?"

He scrunches his face. "Yep. We watch football on Sundays anyway, not baseball."

Trey is playing against the Bombers up in New York today. While all the New York fans still love him, they *hate* me. I'm blamed for Trey leaving the team. I don't go to many away games, but New York would be an easy away game for me to attend given its proximity to Philly. I tried to go once at the beginning of the season, but security had to escort me from my seat to a private box because of all the hate I was getting. People were legitimately throwing beer cans at me.

Trey freaked out, and I haven't been back since, but it doesn't prevent them from holding up signs along the lines of *she's no GEM, please come back*. Trey doesn't like me to even watch the games in New York.

He, on the other hand, has become the poster child for women's rights groups due to his speech, which went viral.

I shrug. "Some of the signs are actually funny. It doesn't bother me anymore."

Okay, it bothers me a little bit. I didn't ask him to leave the team. Why am I being blamed?

CJ holds up another slice of pizza for me, but I hold up my hand. "No, no, no. I have a wedding dress to fit into in six weeks. No more pizza for me."

"It's spinach and tomato. It's vegetables. It's practically healthy."

"Dammit. You're an asshole." I hold out my hand. "Give it to me."

He chuckles. "So easy to tempt you. You're going to be a beautiful bride no matter what. Eat up."

"Thank you. And you two will be the most beautiful brides-maids ever."

We all laugh. Val and CJ are in my bridal party. They bought pale pink suits to match the bridesmaid dresses. Not an easy color for them to find, but they were determined to do so. Grammy Jane is my maid of honor, with Trey's sister, her wife, Libby, JoJo, Ava, and Taylor rounding out my bridal party.

My mother initially started planning the wedding, but I had to take all responsibility away from her. She was driving me nuts, and Trey hated how stressed it was making me. He diplomatically managed to make it seem like he was doing a favor for my mother by taking the reins.

Trey and I are now doing everything ourselves, and we couldn't be happier. It's going to take place just after the season is over. I'm counting the seconds until he's my husband.

After watching two full football games, I look at my watch as I stretch and yawn. "It's getting late. Trey should be home soon.

I'm going to get going. You know, I gotta…make the bed and stuff."

CJ raises an eyebrow. "Don't bullshit us. You just want to get home so you can get railed."

I smile widely. "Three days is a long time to go without my fiancé. I've missed him. And when he returns from a road trip, the sex is off the charts. Well, it's always off the charts with him, but there's that reuniting element when he returns." I shiver. "So hot."

They both roll their eyes, and I giggle. They hate hearing about my sex life with Trey. So of course I give them *very* specific details anytime I can.

I say goodbye and begin my walk home. I'm a few blocks from my house when I receive a text notification. Looking down at my phone, I notice that it's from that same unknown number from all those months ago.

I open the text and it's a picture of me…from about thirty seconds ago. What? I snap my head around, and before I know what's happening, a big hand covers my mouth, followed by an arm wrapping around me and then pulling me a few steps into a nearby alley.

I'm about to scream when a familiar scent invades my nostrils. I mumble into the hand, "Trey?"

I hear him chuckle as he removes his hand. I turn around in his arms while otherwise being pinned to a brick wall. I narrow my eyes at him. "Has it been you all along?"

He smiles. "You said you wanted to try the stalker trope. Cheetah helped me with the original pics to make sure you didn't suspect me."

I twist my lips. "Hmm. I did say that, but it's not as fun in reality. You scared the shit out of me."

He cages me in and rubs his massive erection against my center. "I don't know. It's kind of hot. Maybe I'll tie you up and have my wicked way with you."

I squirm against him until he's rubbing the right spot. Wrapping my arms around his neck, I say, "I'm all for the BDSM trope, but let's leave the felony tropes to the romance novels." I softly kiss his lips. "Tell me more about what your wicked way would entail. Be detailed about what's on this…menu."

He slowly licks up my neck. "Well, the restaurant is called Trey's Trope Trattoria."

Ooh, I like this game. "I've never heard of it."

He runs his hand under my loose skirt, slides my panties to the side, and dips a finger inside me. Bringing it back out to his mouth and licking it, he says, "Such a good amuse-bouche."

I smile. "My bouche is very amused."

"For the full appetizer, you'll spread your long legs for me, right here in public, while I feed my cock into your pretty pussy."

He unzips his jeans and pulls out his cock before lifting me and making good on his promise by sliding in deep. So deep.

Once inside me, he stills as we both adjust to the sensation that's been vacant the past few days. I've missed the closeness. He squeezes my ass, letting me know he's feeling the same.

I breathe, "An appetizer of the expeditionist trope is top-notch. What else does Trey's Trope Trattoria offer?"

After beginning his movements inside me and kissing along my jaw, he whispers, "The intermezzo will be when I come inside you and then feed it to you."

I can't help but giggle. "Ooh, a little semen soufflé. Cum-play is a good trope and certainly a delicious palette cleanser. I'm liking this restaurant so far."

He establishes a rhythm inside me. I throw my head back. "Oh god, that's good. Keep talking. I love when you talk to me."

"The main course will be at home when I serve you a heavy dose of the BDSM trope. I'm going to tie your wrists and ankles to our bed and lather you in what's inside the lavender *and* fuchsia bottles."

"What about the apricot-colored bottle?"

"That too, but first I'll need an accompaniment."

I grin. "And what's the appropriate accompaniment for a main meal of BDSM?"

"It consists of feasting on your pussy and bringing you to the edge over and over again, not letting you fall over until I decide it's time."

I mock gasp. "The edging trope is hot. Only the most skilled chefs can make it happen though. Is the chef at Trey's Trope Trattoria that good?"

We smile into each other's mouths. Trey has edged me multiple times with explosive success.

"You know he is. He's an expert inside Gemma's kitchen. It's his favorite kitchen."

I deadpan, "It's the *only* kitchen for him."

He nods as he thrusts in and out of me. "Only one he'll ever want."

His cock inside me feels so damn good. I breathe into his mouth, "I've missed you."

He breathes back, "I feel like a part of me is missing when we're not together."

Our playful banter is momentarily stopped as my emotions overcome me. That's exactly how it feels when he's gone. Like I'm incomplete. Ugh, I'm such a cheesy, madly in love, female main character from one of my books.

I moan, "More. Give me more information on the menu."

He slowly moves in and out of me. "While the appetizer is gentle lovemaking, the main course will include fucking you hard and deep. You won't know where I end and you begin. It won't conclude until you've had several orgasms. Your hot little pussy will explode on my cock over and over again."

"Oh fuck." His actions and words tip me into oblivion. I tilt my head back as my world goes momentarily dark. My legs shake, and my orgasm takes over my entire body.

I hear him groan as he pumps into me a few more times and spills himself inside me.

After a few breathless moments, I ask, "What's on the dessert menu at Trey's Trope Trattoria?"

He bites my neck as he grabs my ass. "Peach Gobbler."

I let out a laugh. "Peach Cobbler?"

He squeezes me a few more times. "Nope. Gobbler."

I kiss his lips and run my fingers through his hair. "I love Trey's Trope Trattoria. I'm giving it a five-star review."

He smiles into my mouth. "The best part of Trey's Trope Trattoria is the happily ever after."

THE END

WANT a glimpse into Gemma and Trey's future? The extended epilogue can be found here:

Acknowledgments

To Gemma and Trey: You two were so refreshing to write after the emotions of writing Ripley and Quincy's story. Gemma, I love your strength and character. Trey, I love the way you love Gemma. I'm so happy I get to continue writing you two in the Extra Innings series.

To the Queen, TL Swan: You are the reason everything I write exists. You're also the reason I met my author besties.

To Lakshmi, Thorunn, Mindy, and Brittany: Thank you for being the best beta bitches a girl could ever hope for, but, most of all, thank you for being my friends.

To My OG Beta Readers Stacey and Fun Sherry: Thank you for being there for me since day one. You've been my biggest and hottest cheerleaders every single step of the way.

To The B!tch Squad Members: Thank you all for supporting me and loving my books. You keep me going in this crazy journey.

To Chrisandra and K.B. Designs: **Chrisandra**: Thank you for making me feel illiterate. That's what makes you such a great editor. **Kristin**: Thank you for helping this artistically challenged woman. Thank you for creating covers with specific instructions from me like, "Do what you think is best."

To My Family: I truly feel bad for you. An immature mother and wife can't be easy. To my daughters, thank you for tolerating me (ish). Thank you for telling everyone you know that your mom writes sex books. I appreciate that by the time you were each six, you were more mature than me. To my handsome husband, thank you for your blind support. You never question my sanity, which can't be easy. But let's face it, you do reap the benefits of the fact that I write sex scenes all day long. Every single male main character has a little of you in him (only the good stuff - wink wink).

About the Author

AK Landow lives in the USA with her husband, three daughters, one dog, and one cat (who was chosen because his name is Trevor). She enjoys reading, now writing, drinking copious amounts of vodka, and laughing. She's thrilled to have this new avenue to channel her perverted sense of humor. She is also of the belief that Beth Dutton is the greatest fictional character ever created.

AKLandowAuthor.com

City of Sisterly Love Series

Knight: Book 1 Darian and Jackson

Dr. Harley: Book 2 Harley and Brody

Cass: Book 3 Cassandra and Trevor

Daulton: Book 4 Reagan and Carter

About Last Knight: Book 5 Melissa and Declan

Love Always, Scott: Prequel Novella Darian and Scott

Quiet Knight: Novella Jess and Hayden

Belles of Broad Street Series

Conflicting Ventures: Book 1 Skylar and Lance

Indecent Ventures: Book 2 Jade and Collin

Unexpected Ventures: Book 3 Beth and Dominic

Enchanted Ventures: Book 4 Amanda and Beckett

Extra Innings Series

Double Play: Arizona and Layton

CurveBall: Ripley and Quincy

Payoff Pitch: Bailey and Tanner

Off Season: Kamryn and Cheetah

Faking the Book Boyfriend: Gemma and Trey (Being published as part of the Book Boyfriend Builders collaboration)

Signed Books: aklandowauthor.com